MAD MAMA IN SHATTERED DREAMS

BRENDA K. NEULIEB

MAD MAMA IN SHATTERED DREAMS

TATE PUBLISHING
AND ENTERPRISES, LLC

Mad Mama in Shattered Dreams
Copyright © 2014 by Brenda K. Neulieb. All rights reserved.

No part of this publication may be reproduced, stored in a retrieval system or transmitted in any way by any means, electronic, mechanical, photocopy, recording or otherwise without the prior permission of the author except as provided by USA copyright law.

The opinions expressed by the author are not necessarily those of Tate Publishing, LLC.

Published by Tate Publishing & Enterprises, LLC
127 E. Trade Center Terrace | Mustang, Oklahoma 73064 USA
1.888.361.9473 | www.tatepublishing.com

Tate Publishing is committed to excellence in the publishing industry. The company reflects the philosophy established by the founders, based on Psalm 68:11,
"The Lord gave the word and great was the company of those who published it."

Book design copyright © 2014 by Tate Publishing, LLC. All rights reserved.
Cover design by Rtor Maghuyop
Interior design by Mary Jean Archival

Published in the United States of America
ISBN: 978-1-63122-087-6
1. Fiction / Mystery & Detective / Women Sleuths
2. Fiction / Thrillers / Crime
14.02.18

Dedication

Thanks to Gail Vincent for believing in me; for Laura Tarasoff's editing help; for my children, John, Joey, and Joshua, who encouraged me the whole time; and, finally, my husband, Joe, who helped in the end to make *Mad Mama* a successful novel. Thanks, everyone! But most of all, thank you, Jesus, for giving me this story!

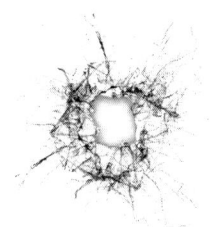

Introduction

The house was hushed. Everyone was still asleep except for Mona, who was restless. Her eyes were wide awake as she lay on the bed tossing her 120-pound body from one side of the king size mattress to the other side. She rolled around all night having nightmare after nightmare, reliving horrifying events that actually took place only yesterday. They tormented her mind regularly during the night and almost every waking hour of the following morning.

Being annoyed of the lack of sleep she acquired, Mona sprang up from her sleigh bed, threw off the downy filled comforter, and promptly headed toward the kitchen just down the hall about twenty tiny feet away. "I'll just read the newspaper and enjoy another one of those beautiful sunrises," she convinced herself, trying not to think of the past recollections that remained constant on her mind and put her sleep in a disarray. But no matter how hard she tried to dismiss them, little by little the dreaded scenes continued forcing their way back through her thoughts.

Mona still insisted on essaying to relax and enjoying her usual morning tryst with God, so she grabbed a cup of steaming hot coffee and marched confidently into the living room. Standing back inside the shadows, Mona gazed out of the bay windows as if she were in a trance. Waiting for the sunrise to burst out its inspirational glow, she tried to focus on pleasant remembrances, while pushing back the unwanted ones. Finally, what she had longed for just arrived. The premature morning opened the new day with a warm glowing light that pierced its way through the bay windows of Mona's two-story home. As she stood back within the silhouettes and watched, the rays of the warm sunlight eased her mind. Then the horizon lit up with a golden spray that surrounded the skies with pink and blue highlights.

This is going to be a wonderful day, thought Mona, *I can just feel it.* Yet her peaceful sunrise turned sour when once again recollections of yesterday pushed back into her thoughts. She strived to hide them and enjoy the beginning of a beautiful, brand-new day. Taking a deep breath, Mona firmly tightened her grip on the handle of the coffee mug she was holding and sipped some of the hot brew. A mist of steam brushed against her reflective pale face, and a cold chill rushed throughout Mona's entire body.

"Get a grip, Mona," she commanded herself as flashbacks continued to haunt and tease her. Then she grabbed the morning edition of the *Sun Valley Newspaper* that she had been clutching underneath her arm and opened it hoping to introduce new thoughts, and read away her problems. As she read the title page, she gasped, "Oh, my gosh!" To her amazement, there she stood, the cover story, wearing her military green attire, heavily armed from head to toe and in a high kick position. Then suddenly, like a faucet that couldn't be turned off, the unwanted flashbacks began gushing forth, surfacing so quickly they seemed to be out of control.

"That was real? I actually did that…and with a grenade? Oh, my baby! Oh, please, God, I don't want to relive this again," she said pausing in between each sentence. Yesterday's memories were too disturbing for Mona's mind to stay serene. "I must have been mad and out of my mind," she continued. "I risked the lives of my family and my children. How did it get so far out of control?" she wondered incessantly. "Why won't my mind let go of these past events? *It is over*, isn't it?"

With her eyes staring up into the heavens, she cried aloud, yet softly as to not awaken her family, "God, is there a reason why I'm supposed to keep remembering all this? Maybe it's not over yet. Maybe I missed something. What could it be? Tell me, please."

There were too many unanswered questions. Mona knew the past events were going to continue haunting her mind until she surrendered. Boldly, she turned away from the bay windows and faced the living room. "All right, that's it! I give up! What did I miss?" she spoke abruptly and out loud as if she were speaking to someone in the room. "I won't stifle my memories from coming through any longer. And maybe then," she pondered, "I can put an end to this nightmare and my heart, mind, body, and soul can finally get some rest."

Therefore, in order to analyze the whole event from the very start, Mona began to recall the beginning chapters of such an audacious, unbelievable venture in her life that just refused to be forgotten.

The first chapter begins with Mona's family.

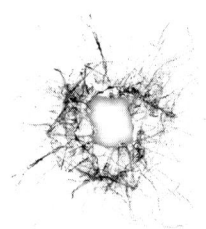

CHAPTER 1

THE FAMILY

The alarm in Mona's bedroom disquietingly demanded her to awaken. It rang out loud and nonstop, annoying Mona greatly. She reached over and gave it a hard slap, then went back to sleep. It wasn't but minutes later Mona slapped the alarm again. She continued punching the alarm button three consecutive times more as the wake-up calls persistently urged her to awaken. "Just five more minutes!" she kept yelling at the clock, as if it were agitating her purposely. Five more minutes for Mona turned into another hour. The alarm rang again, but this time Mona made an effort to turn over and face her foe. With a squint of her eyelids to peak open Mona's olive-green eyes, she tried to focus in on the illuminated numbers of her clock face. Completely surprised at the time, she quickly pushed off the alarm button and forced her sleepy-eyed body to a standing position. With half-opened eyes, Mona attempted to step into one leg of her jeans, stumbled, and fell sideways onto the bed.

"I can do this," she assured herself, and her next attempt was a little more successful. Mona grabbed a blue T-shirt with the words, "I am the Mama! Get back!" embroidered on the front side and "Cause I've Been Trained to Kick" embroidered on the backside. She pulled it down over her head with force and punched her arms through the sleeves as she exited the doorway. Then Mona dashed into the kitchen. In order to make up for lost time, Mona tried to rush the food arrangements. She began tossing food onto the countertops, banging pots and pans and clanging dishes against each other. "Be quiet," she reminded herself knowing the noise would cause her children to awaken. Mona stopped working long enough to fill an empty coffee pot with four cups of water and some even measures of ground coffee. She plugged it into a nearby electrical outlet and then went back to her dinner preparations. While the coffee brewed, the aroma traveled up Mona's sensitive nostrils. She could hardly wait for the first cup, but while waiting, she began preparing the main course for her Christmas dinner.

Mona stuffed a twenty-pound precooked turkey with her own sage-stuffing recipe that her younger brother titled "A La Stuff It." After stuffing the naked beast and placing it into a cooking bag, Mona then placed it into a large pan and shoved it into the oven, slamming the door abruptly. Hurriedly, Mona gathered ingredients for the other dishes. When the last one was prepared, she rushed to the coffee pot to enjoy the morning with peace and serenity. Mona knew it wouldn't be long until her three children would awaken, and as for the silence, well, it would be completely erased from one of her most favored activities of the morning.

Before long, the distinctive smells of sage stuffing, roasting turkey, and rolls blended together and drifted upstairs to the three bedrooms where Mona's boys were sleeping. They arose from their slumber sniffing heavily. Still in pajamas, each child followed behind the other, forming a single line down the staircase.

"Hmm," sniffed John, the eldest. "Something smells good enough to eat." John, approaching the age of eighteen and even though he had such a hearty appetite, was able to maintain a six-foot slender profile.

"Me too!" exclaimed Joey, the middle child. He paused, thought a second, and commented briefly, "I wonduh if it's snowin' outside!" Joey loved being close to nature's surroundings more than he loved eating. However, unlike his brother John, at four feet and forty-five pounds heavy, Joey's physique showed a little bulge around his waist and chubby little cheeks. He didn't mind though; he liked being substantial because for a six-year-old, Joey was very stout. It made him feel important when his uncle Willie denoted him Mighty Joe.

The four-year-old, Joshua (soon to be five in six months), very clever for his young age and also lean in appearance like his brother John, silently followed along behind Joey's lead with both eyes shut. Sporadically, he would take a quick peek so he could watch for loose obstacles that were left out on the floor.

"Watch out for the huge bug on your way down," warned brother John.

"That's not a bug, John. It's a bee," Joshua managed to debate as he squinted open one eye and pushed the toy out of his way with his right bunny slipper foot.

"Yeah, so it's still a bug."

"No, it's not. Bugs have eight legs, bees have six. That makes it an insect, not a bug."

"Excuse me, Mr. Science Professor. It won't matter what it is, if mom sees it on the stairs."

"Shush, John, I'll put it away after breakfast," he warned with his right palm stretched upward like a traffic cop and his eyes bulged out like a bullfrog. Both of the older boys laughed at his humorous face.

"Josh," laughed Joey, "you yook funny."

"Nonetheless, I have a mission."

Laughing John asked, "What kind of mission is that, Josh?"

Josh looked at his older brother and replied, "If I tell you, you'll get there before me, and my mission will be a bust."

The boys laughed and continued climbing down the flight of steps. The kitchen, of course, was the main source of the smell that guided their noses down the stairs. Upon their arrival to the entrance of the kitchen, the eldest male child peeked around the door in an attempt to secretly spy on his mother. "*Sh*, quiet," John whispered, "let's sneak up and scare the condiments out of mom."

"Okay," the other two brothers agreed trying not to giggle out loud.

John arranged his brothers according to their height, one head standing directly above and behind the other head with their left shoulders leaning against the side post. The youngest stood first in line at the bottom of their makeshift totem pole. Next came the middle child, Joey, and then John stood behind the other two arranging his head at the top. Then to hold a statue position, John wrapped his arms around the younger brothers. The youngest children stifled their sniggering and watched Mom perform her morning activities.

Mona poured herself a cup of hot, black coffee and added some cream and sugar. She picked up a spoon from off the counter top and stirred briskly. Lifting the cup to take a sip, she turned and headed for the kitchen table. A totem pole replica of three heads each with smiling faces and six reaching arms popped out at her. Mona jumped and spilled her coffee on the kitchen floor.

"Boys! You startled me," she gasped for breath. They laughed.

"Gotcha, Mom, didn't we?" asked the little one.

"You sure did, sweetie," Mona agreed and tickled Joshua's belly that was exposed from an unbuttoned part in his nightshirt. He giggled and then remembered why he came downstairs.

"Mom, is it time to eat? It sure smells good," asked Joshua as he began his usual lengthy one-way conversation. "I like what you cook, Mom. Have you been up all night working on this *wonderful* smell?" he continued as he gestured with his peewee-sized hands.

"Josh!" Mona interrupted as she bent over to clean up her spill. "It'll be awhile yet."

"Oh, man! Mom! I'm starving. I need something now!" grumbled John who is always ready for the next meal.

"Don't worry, John. I knew you out of everyone else in this house would be hungry, so I baked crescent rolls to tie you over until dinner."

"Crescents! That's the smell that woke me up."

"Great. I knew I should've waited to bake those rolls." Mona moaned with half a smile as she glanced over to the counter that supported a pan full of crescent rolls.

"All right, Mom! You're the greatest. Don't worry, we won't get in your way," John gladly exclaimed and disappeared for a short while with a couple of crescent rolls in each hand and a few extras tucked away in the pockets of his pants.

"Hey, gweedy, yeave some for us," whined Joey.

"I made plenty, Joey."

Joey grabbed a handful of rolls and swiftly headed for the back door. He stopped suddenly in his steps, turned around, and faced his mother with a sinister smile and asked, "Mom, can I go outside until its weady?" Even though his speech was getting clearer and the sounding of his consonants were getting better, Joey still had a few words that weren't understandable. Mona spent a lot of time helping Joey with his phonics, which left less time for the other boys, so she tried whatever technique worked better and faster. Therefore, through experimentation and observation, Mona found the perfect solution to motivate Joey was being outdoors. Whenever Joey had homework or needed practice on his speech, she would make every effort possible to work with him outdoors, weather permitting, of course. Joey was quite aware of this procedure and was positive his mother would allow him to escape outside for just about anything.

As he suspected, Mona allowed his request, and in a flash, he disappeared out the back door. Joshua grabbed handfuls as well and followed the procession behind his middle-aged brother. John returned for more, loaded up his pockets once again, and exited the kitchen with a great slam to the back door. Mona noticed John had changed into jeans, but the younger boys ran outside in their pajamas.

"Hey you two run upstairs and change. Make sure you put on warm clothes."

Jumping back into her relaxed state, Mona immediately sat down on one of the kitchen chairs enjoying her morning coffee with solitude and a quick sigh of relief. "Hmm, that worked out pretty good. I wonder how long though," she said with a half a smile.

It wasn't long though until John flew back into the kitchen again for the third time; only, he wasn't filling up his pockets with rolls. This time, he was in a state of distress. "Mom," he whined, standing broad shouldered with a cute baby-smooth face that tended to pout as he spoke.

"What is it, honey?" Mona tried to sound understanding, but her mind had escaped so far back in time; she wasn't sure if she could return back to the present so quickly. She was enjoying her relaxed state all too much.

"Mom, are you listening to me?"

"Huh, oh, I'm sorry, John. What were you saying?"

"Joey bent the rim on my front tire!"

"Let me see." Mona stood up and quickly inspected her son's damaged bicycle rim that was dangling from his hand. There seemed to be only one conclusion. "Well," she said with a straight face, "looks like we'll have to shoot it."

"Mom, I don't know what you mean, but that's not funny. I have a bicycle tournament coming up soon. I need this fixed before the beginning of next week or I won't be able to compete."

Mona smiled and said with a short chuckle, "We use to say that all the time when I was growing up." John wasn't smiling. "Uh, never mind. Sorry," Mona said as she cleared her throat, "old joke." Quickly changing the subject as well as the melody in her voice, Mona said, "Let me see what you have here, John." Looking down at the rim that John was holding, Mona asked with puzzlement, "John, how did this happen?" She grabbed the crooked bicycle part from her son's right hand and turned it around from side to side. "I know Joey is strong, but he's not capable of bending it like this."

"He was riding on it and fell off. The bicycle soared into the back wheels of Mr. Sardy's town car."

"He what? Is he all right? Where is he?" Mona panicked and darted toward the back door and began yelling.

"Joey! Are you okay?" she yelled on her way out the door.

"Mom, mom, relax, he's okay," John yelled trying to get his mother to stop moving and listen. "Mom, only the bicycle was damaged. Joey wasn't even on it."

"Oh," Mona said as she sighed with much relief, returned to the kitchen, and sat back down in one of the kitchen chairs to calm down.

"But, Mom, he didn't even try to save the bike when he fell. He just laid there as it rolled down the sidewalk, and he watched it fall over flat on the ground behind Mr. Sardy's town car," John explained the whole story to his mother. Then he ended the story with his head hanging low and his head shaking from side to side, then sadly announced, "Then Mr. Sardy backed over it. It was sure destruction."

"I see," she said, trying not to laugh as her son dramatized the scene. With a little further inspection, Mona came to a quick decision. "I don't think it can be repaired, John, but it can be replaced with a new one, when the stores are open."

"What? When can we do that? All the stores are closed. I need it now."

"John, the mall will be open tomorrow until about noon. I have to run by there tomorrow to pick up something for Willie, so I'll just drop by the bicycle shop and pick up a new rim for you. How's that?"

"You mean if they have one. That shop never orders extras. I guess that'll have to do. He makes me so mad. Joey always breaks my things. I wish I didn't have a stupid little brother," John strongly admitted as he charged out of the room.

"John!" yelled Mona. "Oh, for goodness sakes," she sighed.

"Joey," Mona yelled out the back door again, "get in here!"

"Mama." Joey quickly ran in to transfer the blame, with his little brother, Josh, right in behind him. "I didn't do it. Josh was playing with it too. He could have done it."

"I did not, stupid!" he said directing an insult to his older brother.

"Mama, Joey did it. I saw him do it. He's lucky he wasn't still on it when it crashed into Mr. Sardy's car," Josh announced quickly to reverse the blame that was placed upon him.

"You didn't see it cwash, dumby. You were way on the other side of the house. You'wa just on John's side, idiot."

"I am not, stupid, shut up."

"You gonna make me, yitta baby?"

"Hey, you two, cut it out," Mona reprimanded.

Mona turned to Joey with a little hope that she'd figured out the puzzle. "Joey, if Joshua was on the other side of the house, how could he have crashed John's bike?"

"Yeah, Joey, what about that?"

Joey hung his head quietly but, without a moment's notice, lifted up his bowed head and sprang out with the words, "He... uh." But at a loss for words, sprang out with, "It's not my fau't. Mr. Sa'dy's ca' hit it afta I fell off. I didn't bweak it!" Joey yelled loud so his elder brother could hear. "Stupid o' John. He just wants me to get into twouble. He awways bwames me for evwything of his that bwakes. Anyway, I couldn't stop it fwom ro'ing into the ca'."

Of course, the oldest that had been eavesdropping in the next room couldn't stay away any longer. John ran back into the kitchen and loudly but briefly explained, "I do not blame you for everything of mine that breaks! And you could have stopped it from rolling into Mr. Sardy's car. You could've gotten up, stupid. You just laid there and laughed about it."

All three siblings proceeded to loudly debate. The disputes of "No, I couldn't!" and "Yes, you could, stupid!" bounced back and forth until Mona couldn't hold her temper any longer.

"*Stop!*" yelled Mona louder than she had ever yelled. She got their attention quickly though. The three boys, very much amazed, turned and looked straight at their mother. Not knowing the outcome of her sudden upheaval, each boy remained motionless and speechless until they felt it was safe to do so again.

Mona simply smiled, glared at her middle son, Joey, and softly patted him on the back. "When you borrow something from someone, you are responsible for anything that happens to it, while it is in your possession. Therefore, tomorrow," she said, "I'll purchase another rim with the money you have saved already and the money you will make by doing odd jobs around the house during the holidays."

"No, that's not fair. It wasn't my fau't," demanded Joey, and the bickering started all over again. "Nobody yikes me in this famye. I just wun away."

"Ha!" John darted. "You always say that, stupid, but you never do it."

"You're stupid!" Joey retorted, sticking out his well-rounded tongue directly at John and adding another ugly facial expression right behind it.

"Quiet!" yelled Mona with repeated authority. Once again, the boys remained speechless. "Now, the three of you go to the den and don't come back into this kitchen for anything. *Do you hear me?*" Mona paused a moment and then raised her voice again with the last word receiving the highest pitch. "*And stop calling each other stupid!*"

The boys reluctantly walked out of the kitchen with discontent and lowly mumbled bickering sounds all the way to the den. Mona returned to her dinner preparations, and about the time she was elbow deep into her work, the doorbell rang. Not knowing what to do with her messy hands, she yelled for instant help.

"Would someone, please, get the door. My hands are a mess," Mona yelled forcefully from behind the kitchen wall. Her loud rebounding voice ricocheted off the kitchen wall and the sound waves danced all the way to the den. Her efforts were not rewarded though because neither of the boys made a move to open the front door.

Mona yelled again, only this time she added an effective motivation, "It may be Uncle Willie!" As soon as she yelled out those two magic words, sparks began to fly. Each boy jumped up from their seats and charged promptly for the front door.

"Oh, wow, Uncle Willie! I'll answer the door," exclaimed John.

"Oh, no, you won't, John. You ansud it the yast time," disagreed Joey.

"Mom told me to, stupid."

"She did not. She said someone, and you'ah not a someone. You'ah not even a somebody."

"Then what am I?"

"We', if you don't know what you ah', how do you aspect me to know, huh?"

While the two older siblings squabbled over personal matters and made faces at each other, the youngest ran to the door and opened it without question. "Oh, it's only Aunt Mildred," Josh announced with disappointment. Mildred popped in quickly before Joshua closed the door back in her face.

"Hi, Aunt Mildred," said Josh in an "unhappy to see you" expression. The other two boys moped back toward the den.

"Gee," Mildred expressed her gratitude to Mona who was wiping her wet hands on a hand towel, "they couldn't wait to see me, could they?"

Mona gave her sister a hug and began to apologize for the boys' rude behavior. Before Mona could say one word of apology though, Mildred sang out melodiously, "Hey, boys! Look who I brought with me."

As soon as their favorite uncle poked his head around the door, both the younger children yelled in unison, "Hooray, it's Uncle Willie!"

"Yes!" exclaimed John with both fists clinched and two thumbs up.

Uncle Willie stepped his six-and-a-half foot, 250-pound body inside the house and closed the front door. He reached over to give his big sister a hug and stated sarcastically, "We would have been here sooner, sis, but Mildred had a burger attack. We had to drive fifteen miles out of our way just to find the right restaurant."

"It was not fifteen miles," explained Mildred, interrupting their conversation, "and anyway, that's my favorite place to eat. You both know that." Mildred's long, brassy red hair lit up her rosy, red cheeks as she tried to defend her actions. She too, being slender in profile, had a secret like John to eat all she wanted and not even show a hint of the basic bulge. Also like John, Mildred was always hungry.

"Mildred," thought Mona out loud, "aren't you eating here for dinner? I could have slept in this morning and saved a few extra lives on my alarm clock. I know I must have killed it at least five times this morning." Mona spoke calmly at first, but her voice began to rise excitedly as she continued to discipline Mildred's rash behavior and began poking her finger into Mildred's chest. "Mildred, you know I cook more, because you and John eat more." Mona grabbed the collar of Mildred's blouse and jokingly continued with a snarl, "Mildred, why did you eat, when you knew I was *cooking*?"

"Mona." Mildred shirked. "Did the boys get up too early and make you miss your coffee break this morning?"

"Mona," interrupted Uncle Willie, "you can relax. She didn't go there to eat."

"Oh," Mona said, releasing Mildred's collar, and straightening it with a smirk, "but, Willie, you said she had a burger attack."

"Yeah, well, that was her excuse at first just to get me to drive there, and may I attempt to say this once again," Willie remarked with a little sassy sarcasm as he turned toward Mona.

"Yes, you may," agreed Mona.

"Thank you. We went way out of our way to stand in a long line"—he extended his arms widely—"of bratty kids so we could get a personal autographed picture from you know who at that favorite place she likes to eat. Of course, we both know that."

Willie and Mona glared at Mildred with a "Well, what do you have to say for yourself?" look. Mildred, finally getting a chance to speak up, just shrugged her shoulders and smiled dumbfounded. She figured speaking would only worsen matters, so she kept silent.

The sibling query lasted longer than Mona's boys were willing to wait. Each younger child tugged at their uncle's arms in an attempt to maneuver him toward the den. Willie finally gave in to their persistence and allowed the boys to impel him to move forward. Quickly in the struggle, Willie reached down to retrieve a large bag he had placed on the floor upon his arrival. He was then swiftly pushed from behind and pulled from the front. The children strained with all their might. As soon as Willie unstinted his lock, he marched away smartly with his head held high, a smile on his oval face, and complete joy in his heart. Uncle Willie turned to take a quick look at his two sisters and remarked, "What can I say? They love me." He then disappeared into the shadows with John tagging along behind.

"What is it with him anyway?" asked Mildred. "You'd think he carried a chocolate factory underneath his jacket with the way they carry on about him."

"Oh, sis, don't take it so hard. They became attached to Willie after Jorge's death. They need him right now."

"Attached? You make them sound like little sea urchins," Mildred chuckled.

"Mildred, you're always joking. Come on, let's go finish dinner. I've got some last-minute touches to do."

"Oh, yes, how could I forget the famous Mona and her most beautiful entrées that no one sees, but me. Honestly, Mona, I don't understand why you spend so much time decorating the food." Then Mildred chanted with a soprano voice sounding like one of the old cooking show hostesses, while she pictured some of Mona's dishes, "Potato salad with egg slices arranged neatly on top, a sprinkle or two of paprika topped off with olive halves. Oh, and we must not forget those darling celery trees to garnish," she sang. "And then," she continued her song, "the stuffing is garnished with those cute little celery trees and more egg slices sprinkled with paprika, also for added eye appeal." Mildred smiled sweetly, cocked her head to the left, blinked her eyelashes three times and said, "You know, I feel I'm in heaven when I eat here."

Mona laughed. "Very funny. You know how much I enjoy decorating."

"I'm shocked you haven't decorated the celery trees with ornaments yet."

"Hey, I never thought of that."

"Great. Mona, don't you realize it's a complete waste of your time. What you take hours preparing, this family takes milliseconds to destroy, and they don't even appreciate your efforts. Why bother?"

"They may not appreciate it, Mildred, but I do. It gives me a good feeling inside—you know completeness."

Mildred looked at the bare dining room table and commented, "Well, I can decorate the dinner table and then"—Mildred clasped her hands together and swayed her body from left to right making a high-pitched, melodious voice once again—"and then…I can feel good inside too, Mona dearest."

Mona laughed again and said, "Mildred, you're so silly, but you can't."

"And why not? You don't like the way I do it?"

"No, it's because that's Joey's job tonight."

"Come on, sis. Do you really think you're gonna drag him away from his lovable Uncle Willie? Face it, sis, I'm all you've got."

"Yeah, I guess you're right." Clasping her hands together and lifting them against her chest, Mona remarked jokingly, "Well, then, sister dear, I suppose you can feel good inside too," she said, and then with her right arm flowing downward and stretched out toward the dining room, Mona bowed slightly and continued with, "Be my guest to complete yourself as you garnish the dining room table."

"Ha," Mildred scoffed as she walked into the dining room and began setting the dishes and silverware on the table. Mona returned to her dinner creations. Soon Mildred parted from the dining room and joined Mona in the kitchen. She filled the kitchen sink with hot water, dishwashing liquid, and any dirty dishes she found laying around. While the dishes were soaking, Mildred tied up the garbage bag and took it outside for pick up. On her return, she began washing the soaking dishes.

"Hey," Mona spoke as she thought, "you know, this reminds me of Mama."

"How does washing dishes and decorating with celery trees remind you of Mama?"

"Funny," Mona gave a short laugh. "I don't know. I guess, because when we were younger, Mama gave us chores to do like this every day. Remember?"

"Yeah, I remember," Mildred agreed in a melancholy expression.

"You know, we learned a lot from Mama. She sure knew what she was doing when she gave us chores—always the right ones too."

"Ha!" said Mildred in disagreement.

"Mildred!"

"Oh, I didn't mean she didn't know what she was doing, but why did I always get stuck doing the dishes? I would have loved doing many other things and would have done a better job at it too. Come to think of it, we would've had more dishes. I broke more dishes than you can imagine. Every time we went to the store, Mama had to replace the ones I broke."

"That's probably why she gave you that job."

"Why? So I wouldn't do a good job or so Mama could buy more dishes?"

"Don't be silly. Think of it this way. If you do only the chores you like, you won't learn much more than what you already know. It's what you don't like to do that makes you learn a lot more, because you have to do them until you get it right, no matter how many mistakes or breaks you make. See?"

Mildred turned her head back and forth in an east and westward direction. "You lost me on that one, sis."

"Look, it's the jobs we don't do best at that we have to achieve a better performance in. You know, try harder." Mona paused a moment. "That's it! I get it! In turn, we learn to be better at other tasks without being afraid of failure, and we appreciate the likeable jobs even more. I understand it now."

"Well, I wish you would explain it to me. I still don't understand."

"Mildred, it's simple, that's why Mama always made me clean up my room. There wasn't a day gone by that she didn't tell me, 'Mona Faye Crumpet, clean up that filthy room of yours. It's a mess. I'll be checking it later, and you better have it cleaned or you won't be going anywhere today.'"

Mildred cocked her head to one side and in a snarled facial expression said, "Yeah, right. Come on, Mona, cleaning up your room is an easy job. You know Mama was always partial to you for some reason. I didn't have any problems keeping my room clean." Mildred paused for a moment and said, "Come to think of it though, your room was always messy."

"That's right, and yours was always clean."

"Hmm, maybe you're right. Maybe Mama wasn't showing favoritism after all."

"Of course not. You know as well as I do that Mama didn't have a favorite. She must have told us a hundred times, 'If you don't…'" Mona started to repeat a quote and Mildred stepped in to help her out.

Together they quoted, "'Like something, you have to practice it over and over and over and over and over again and again until you finally get it right. Got it?'" They also added, "Got it, Mama," laughed heartily and then went back to work with deep smiles held in their faces. For a while, the room remained silent as each sister escaped into the past and remembered their childhood days.

"There, finished," Mona said, suddenly breaking the silence to their memory escape, "let's go open a present."

"What, now?" asked Mildred as she popped back into the present kitchen.

"Sure, why not?"

"Okay, let's go," Mildred said as she and Mona hooked elbows and did a promenade out of the kitchen and into the living room.

"Boys," Mona yelled, "let's open a present."

"Mona, they can't hear you. You'll have to yell louder than that. Don't forget Uncle Willie is here."

"I guess you're right," Mona agreed, but before she could yell the second time, there were loud noises heard throughout the hallway. Much to Mona's amazement, the next sounds to be heard were shouts of praise like "Yeah!" "All right!" and "I'm for that!"

"I don't believe it," Mona exclaimed. "This is definitely a first."

Mona and Mildred sat down on an end section of Mona's brown, five-piece sectional couch. The two younger boys gathered on the floor in front of Uncle Willie's favorite rocking recliner. John, being the oldest, lingered near the Christmas tree to hand out presents.

"Mom," asked John, "can we open Uncle Willie's presents, please?"

"Yeah, yeah, please, Mama, please," pleaded the younger siblings.

"Well," Mona replied and looked over at Willie, "it's not up to me to decide."

"Oh, I don't care. Go ahead," Willie announced. He knew he couldn't say no.

John reached down underneath the synthetic tree branches and pulled out three presents having the same shapes and sizes. The red one belonged to Joey, the green-colored Christmas wrap belonged to Joshua, and the blue wrapped present belonged to John. John distributed the presents among his brothers first and then began to rip open the blue covering on his own package.

The younger boys hastily opened their presents as well, and in an instant, three boxes were unveiled. With no time to waste, each child flipped the box tops open and forced out the contents. Joey pulled out a football uniform, complete with everything a little football player would need. Josh pulled out a complete baseball uniform with everything a little leaguer would need including a bat, four bases, cleats, and a right hand mitt.

"Wow," exclaimed Joshua, "look what I got, Joey."

"Yeah, that's weawy tight," Joey agreed trying to sound big.

"All right," exclaimed John, "thanks, Uncle Willie! I can sure use this next week for that bicycle contest I entered." John held up a complete bicycle uniform with black leather jacket, black leather gloves, helmet, tight black pants with matching shirt, and even black tennis shoes.

As the boys admired their presents, Mona turned and looked piercingly into her baby brother's big brown eyes. "Well," she said, "I'm waiting."

"Waiting?" questioned Willie. "Oh! John, give your mother her present."

"You know what I mean," she said. "These presents came from an expensive store. They're definitely not cheap store bargains. Why the expensive presents this year?"

"Why? Can't I give my favorite nephews expensive gifts?"

"Yes, you can, but only, if you can afford them."

Willie looked at Mona and then grinned widely. "Well, I can afford them, sister dear, you see, I got a raise."

"You got a raise? Willie, that's great!" Mona expressed her joy by reaching over and giving him a big, hearty hug.

"Mr. Williams liked my suggestion about the new mailboxes. Remember the one I told you about? So he put me in charge along with a huge raise."

"That's great, Bubba," said Mildred with surprise, and she reached and gave him a big hug also.

Their precious victory moment was interrupted by three elves that wanted more surprises. "Mom, it's your turn," they yelled.

"Oh, okay," Mona agreed, and she reached out for the package John was gripping tightly in his hands. The package was neatly wrapped in white paper overlaid with shiny silver stars and beautifully decorated with a large sparkling silver bow. Mona didn't want to destroy its beauty, so she broke open the tape and unraveled the wrapping paper as slowly and neatly as possible.

"Mom," demanded John impatiently, "you're not going to do the other presents like that too, are you?"

"Like what, honey?"

"S-ow-yee," exaggerated Joey in a very deep, shallow voice.

"Oh," chuckled Mona, and everyone laughed with her.

Mona picked up some speed and broke open the last of the wrapping. She opened the box top and pulled out a green military camouflage uniform. Included in the package were dog tags and two hollowed out pineapple hand grenades.

"Uh, Willie," she said astonished, "did you make this purchase all by yourself?"

Everyone laughed, and Willie smiled with an exclamation, "But, Mona, it's what everyone's wearing." As soon as he said that, John became so hysterically out of control that he fell to the floor bursting out with laughter.

"Well, Mom," roared John, "do you like your gag gift?"

"Gag? I'm gagged, that's for sure. I'm glad I'm not into high fashion, Willie, there's no telling what you would have bought at that expensive store for me to wear."

Willie then pulled out a small gift and gave it to Mona. "Here, sis," he said, "you will definitely like this one better."

Mona glanced over at the boys as she began to unravel the next present. In very slow motion at first, she grasped the ribbon that was tied around the package and gradually pulled.

"Mom," whined Josh.

Mona smiled deviously at the boys, giggled, and then picked up the pace. Inside the small package was a box within a box. She opened the second box and pulled out a beautiful silver heart locket with a diamond centered in the middle, and the sides trimmed in gold lace. Mona opened the locket carefully. Inside the locket lay a picture of the three boys on one side and a picture of her late husband on the other.

"Mona, I hope that picture doesn't upset you. Jorge wanted me to have the locket engraved and wrapped so he could give it to you on your anniversary. I thought, emotionally, now you would be ready to accept it. I hope I was right."

"Willie," sighed Mona trying to hold back the tears. "This is beautiful. I love it. Your timing couldn't have been better."

Mona read the inscription on the back, "To the greatest wife, mother in the world. With love from your family." With the locket still open, Mona placed it around her neck. "Well, everyone, how does it look?"

"Great, Mom," said John with tenderness.

"Oh, yes, Mona, it does look great," Mildred agreed softly.

The younger boys weren't sure what to say. They pierced their eyes on the small picture of their father and just bobbed their heads up and down somberly with a quick, fake smile that lasted only a moment.

"I miss Daddy, don't you, Joey?" Joshua whispered to Joey.

"Yeah," he said softly since that was all he could manage to say.

Willie motioned to John with a nod to move forward. John also noticed the unhappy faces around the room, so he quickly tried to change the subject and moved on to happier thoughts. John announced, "Aunt Mildred, I believe it's your turn." He reached over to Mildred and handed her a package from under the tree. It ranged about the same size of the boys' packages, but another box was inserted on the top.

Mildred cautiously looked at the package John held out in front of her. "I wonder what this could be," she said. Giving Willie a quick, denying glance, she remarked, "If he's buying uniforms this year, I know which one he picked out for me." Willie just smiled and shrugged his shoulders.

When Mildred opened the bottom gift, her suspicions were correct. She pulled out a clown suit with makeup, a wig, and big clown shoes, not to mention a big red nose. As she opened the box top to the second gift, two flowers rapidly emerged out of the box. Mildred scooped out a hat with two bobbing flowers. Underneath the hat was an autographed picture of her favorite clown.

"I got one after all," she said holding up the picture in her hand.

"Why do you think I tried to discourage you from getting an autograph today?"

"Well, I didn't know you already got me one."

"Willie, you mean to tell me you two went out of your way today just to get an autographed picture of a clown and came back empty handed?"

"Yes, I told you that. Didn't you hear me?"

"I guess I wasn't paying attention."

"Boy, am I glad," Mildred commented. "You almost tore my blouse and poked a whole in my chest. There's no telling what you would have done, if you knew we came back without it."

"Oh, Mildred, I was just teasing you."

"I know," she said and placed the hat on her head so the boys could see the flowers bob back and forth. Everyone watched Mildred's new hat bob around, and the little boys giggled as the sad memories of their father disappeared.

Uncle Willie opened his present last. His gift was more practical than the others though. Willie pulled out a tabletop barbeque grill, utensils, a chef's hat, and a chef's apron that read "Mailmen also do it in bad weather."

"I'm sorry, Willie, this was John's idea. He said it would blend in with the other presents. Now I know why."

"Yeah, I had everyone's costume picked out without hesitation, but when it came time to buy your present, I was totally stumped. I put my right hand man on the job, and he came up with several ideas."

"Okay, what clue led you to a military outfit?"

"None. I just figured you're a take charge kind of woman, so I decided military all the way would work best for you."

"Right, great choice, Willie."

"More, more," hollered the boys, "we want more presents."

Mona reminded them that they had to wait for Santa's arrival before any more were opened, so they all adjourned to the den.

"First one in gets the controls!" announced Willie as he raced toward the television set.

"Oh, no, not this year," Mona announced. "Football has been rained out in our house this season. Anyone planning on watching football will have to go home."

"But, Mom, we are aweady home," informed Joey.

"Well, then I guess we'll have to think of some other place for you to go this year."

"I know," announced Josh with glee, "we can go outside and fly my new kite."

"What new kite, Josh?" Mona questioned.

"John made me and Joey a new kite. We've got a long tail and lots of string. All we need is the wind behind our backs."

"Sorry, little buddy," laughed Willie, "there's no wind outside at all or even a slight breeze."

"I know what we can do," thought Uncle Willie aloud. "Let's practice karate."

"Hey, yeah, can we? Mama, can we?" asked Joey.

"Okay, but don't get too active. I'd like to keep the house in one piece."

"Ah, you know me, Mama, I can contwol mysef," Joey retorted with a big-eyed smile.

"Right," Mona answered with uncertainty.

Willie showed the boys a few tricks in karate. Mona and Mildred joined them and learned a few tricks as well. Mona tried a few practice jumps and high kicks. She didn't mind the kicks much at all, but the jumps were too exasperating for her, so she retired.

"Willie," she gasped for breath to speak as she plopped down on the couch in the den, "when is Mama suppose to get here?"

"Uh," Willie spoke as he fought, "hai-ah, they said about, aieh-ah, twelve o'clock," he recalled as he belligerently staged an attack on his playful foes. Little did he know, they had plans of their own. The two younger siblings sided together a counter attack. Their poor uncle didn't have a chance. Down to the floor he went and stayed there for a while. As he rested momentarily, the boys complained for more action.

"Come on, Uncle Willie," said Joshua, "get up. I want to hit you again."

"You want to hit me again?" Willie repeated as he grabbed Joshua's legs and pulled him down to the floor and began tickling his armpits.

The grandfather clock in the hallway bonged twelve times. A sigh of relief suddenly came over Willie. He knew it was time to quit in-the-house training. "Boys," he gasped. "Time to quit. It's twelve o'clock."

"So. What's so important about twelve o'clock?" asked Joey.

"Grandma's coming to dinner at noon!"

"But it's not noon yet, Uncle Willie, it's twelve o'clock like you said," Josh explained.

"That is twelve o'clock, Josh," John corrected his baby brother quickly.

"But she's not here yet, Uncle Willie, and you promised me you would fight to the finish," Josh replied as he reached over and smacked his uncle with a karate chop and then tackled his left leg holding on with all his might.

"Yes, but Grandma is never late, don't you boys know that?"

"That's right, boys," Mona agreed.

About that time, there were several knocks upon the front door. "Come on boys, let's go see Grandma!" said Willie with excitement in his voice. Joshua, still hanging onto Willie's left leg, was being dragged along as Willie tugged trying to force his way to the living room. Everyone, except for Mona, followed behind Willie as he pulled his leg along the floor like a wounded soldier. Mona moved ahead and reached the destination point beforehand. When she opened the door, not only was her mother at the door waiting but also two sisters, two brothers-in-law, three nieces, and four young nephews. Mona's mother stepped inside, and the others charged the door behind her, squeezing and pushing to get inside the room first.

"Well," Mona said, "come on in everyone." She stepped back and waited for the group to fight their way inside the door. Mona figured as long as her mother was out of the way, eventually, everyone else would make it in safely. After the last relative squeezed inside the front door, they handed Willie their presents, and the adults found a place to rest in the living room, while the nieces and nephews ran in opposite directions to check out the rest of the house, as was their custom.

Willie waited until all the adults were properly seated. He arranged the presents around the tree and then drifted off into a nearby bedroom. Although he never returned, a Santa with his likeness and build returned in his place.

Uncle Willie, now alias Uncle Claus, hung the new decorations on the tree to see who was absent according to their family tradition. Each member of the family, including the young, brought one specific colored and personalized ornament to replace the old ones from the previous Christmas. Willie removed the old, red ornaments from the tree and simultaneously replaced them with the new blue ones for the present year. One oddball red-colored ornament remained hanging. Uncle Claus glanced at the name and hurriedly put away the old decorations.

"I guess Uncle Tom will get the lucky phone call at chow this year," he thought out loud as he searched for Tom's phone number in Mona's address book. When he found the number, Willie placed it open face down on the telephone stand.

"I hope he doesn't have the flu. That's been going around," Mona grieved.

"He's not sick," announced one of the nieces eavesdropping as she passed through. "Mama talked to him yesterday. Ms. Mona, how much longer do we have to wait to eat? I'm starving. All Grandma gave us to eat this morning were crescent rolls," she asked as she snarled up her nose.

Mona and Willie smiled at each other. Mona commented, "That's our mama!"

"Don't worry, Susan, it won't be much longer."

"Okay," she said a little happier and strolled away to the den.

Dinner was soon ready, and everyone hastily lined up at the table with their empty plates for buffet-style dining. The dinner table was spread with fresh salads, steaming hot gravies, heavenly desserts, and, of course, a large twenty-pound turkey surrounded by Mona's famous Turkey "A La Stuff It" dressing. Among the entrées were broccoli with creamy cheese sauce, sweet corn on the cob, whipped mashed potatoes, and grand-sized homemade dinner rolls. The room strongly hinted with mouthwatering aromas. Each family member breathed in deeply to catch the breezes that teased as it swiftly passed their noses. Secretly, two of the adults reached out to grab a floating turkey mirage but quickly pulled away uncompensated.

The waiting was hard, but the victory was fulfilling. Finally, everyone was served and seated at Mona's long dining room table. The noise level in the room became quiet, except for familiar chewing sounds. Sister Alice made sucking noises, when food got caught between her teeth, brother-in-law Bob would belch between forkfuls, Grandma snorted when she took a break for air, and the others made smacking sounds. Even so, no one seemed to be bothered or distracted from the noises around the room. They were too busy trying to devour the mounds piled upon their plates. Each person, young and old, seemed to work quickly gobbling down their food in hopes of getting a second helping, before it was all consumed.

Willie took a few forkfuls to line his stomach and calm his hunger pangs, then went to the telephone that happened to be in the hallway next to the dining room. As he punched in the last two digits of Uncle Tom's number, Willie turned to his audience and raised his voice enough to be heard by everyone. "Okay, everybody get ready," he yelled. The relatives sitting nearby in the next room made a quick attempt to empty their mouths, before Uncle Willie gave the signal for them to speak. Some of them got up and went near the phone so Uncle Tom could hear them better.

"One, two, three, ready...now!" Willie yelled as he took his hand off the receiver and held it up high toward the crowd of family members that were in the next room.

"Merry Christmas, Uncle Tom," they all shouted and then went back to eating. This time, they began chatting and carrying on conversations between bites.

While the meal was being devoured and Willie talked to Uncle Tom on the telephone, a special pair of nephews decided to make everyone aware of their presence, which was their customary personal trait. These menaces, Lonnie and Donnie by name, both had red hair, freckles, and shiny braces on their teeth. It was quite hard to tell them apart. The only way to distinguish one from the other was to look into their eyes. Lonnie's eyes beamed bright blue-green, and Donnie's eyes beamed a beautiful sea green. Of the twins, Lonnie was the inventor, and Donnie was the perfectionist. In simpler terms, whatever Lonnie did, Donnie had to do better.

Lonnie, the two-minute eldest of the twin menaces, decided he was ready to create a little magic trick with Mona's Christmas tree and a long piece of kite string that he had found in the den. Donnie, on the other hand, remained silent and watched for his turn to perfect the artistry.

Mona's Christmas tree, designed by her late husband, was equipped with wheels that enabled the decorator to turn and decorate all sides of the tree, thus filling all bare spots. After the decorations were in place, the wheels could be locked so it wouldn't roll away.

With the mechanics of Mona's Christmas tree in mind, Lonnie took the kite string he found and tied it to the front legs of the Christmas tree. Later, he sneaked over and unlocked all of the wheels and then, inconspicuously, sat down on one of the end sections of the couch located near the punch bowl table that happened to be in front of the telephone stand where Willie was carrying on a conversation with Uncle Tom. Slowly, he pulled the tree forward. The tree rolled a few inches and then stopped. It wouldn't budge any further. Lonnie noticed the rollers were caught on some of the presents, so he motioned for his brother Donnie to loosen the presents so that no one would see him get up again. Donnie secretly walked toward the tree, reached down, and moved all the big presents to the outside of the tree. He then walked back to the couch near the punch bowl table where his brother Lonnie was sitting. Once again, he pulled on the kite string, and the tree began to roll forward.

Donnie, of course, was anxiously waiting for his turn to help. As he watched Lonnie construct his design, hastily, he reached out and jerked the string. The whole tree, abruptly, jarred loose from all the small presents and charged a pathway down the smooth, shiny waxed floor in Mona's living room. The distance between the bay windows and the punch bowl table gave the runaway Christmas tree enough time to gain much speed. When the tree collided with the punch bowl table, it halted with a short stop and a quick jolt. The top of the tree shifted forward, and about twelve ornaments flew off and simultaneously bit the west wall of the open hallway, where Uncle Claus and four other family members were standing.

John was on his way to fill up his plate again when he noticed the craftiness of the twins in the next room. "Duck, everybody, duck!" screamed John frantically.

Pop! Pop! Pop! Pop, pop, pop! Pop! Pop, pop! Pop, pop, pop! sounded twelve explosions one by one above the frightened heads, as each glass bulb bombarded the wall in haste. Everyone inside the dining room screamed when they heard the explosion, but thanks to John's snap warning, the onlookers in the hallway next to the telephone ducked just in time to only hear and not be a part of the crash above their bobbing heads.

After the bulb attack, complete silence filled the room. Being one of the five victims against the west wall made him cautious to arise to a standing position, so Uncle Claus gradually lifted up his head to see if the seasonal war was over.

"Is it over?" he asked.

"Yes," Mona sighed as she ran to help, "you can all stand up now."

As soon as the room was obviously safe again, some of the family members turned and gleamed at the two culprits they accused to be the perpetrators. The twins looked back in innocence as if to say, "How dare you accuse us of such wild behavior?" Their parents didn't give in to their innocence anymore than the rest of their accusers. Mr. and Mrs. Drake immediately got up from their resting positions, and each parent grabbed an arm of a twin. Lonnie and Donnie squirmed and kicked all the way to Mona's nearby bedroom.

"What are you doing?" they each yelled. "We didn't do it." The parents pulled the boys inside the bedroom, and Mrs. Drake turned toward her audience, politely smiled, and closed the door.

Each twin sat down on the edge of the bed. Their father stood back and looked down at their tearful faces. He was a tall, muscular man with deep, sensitive blue eyes. Before he spanked Lonnie first, Mr. Drake spoke to the boys with compassion. He said, "Now, boys, I don't want to spank you, but you know you were wrong. You ruined Mona's Christmas tree, and you could have injured some of the relatives. I can't let you go unpunished because you won't learn the importance of this lesson. You know your mother and I love you both with all our hearts, and it's just as hard for us to punish you as it is for you to have to take the punishment. Don't let there be a next time like this ever again, or the punishment will be more severe, okay?"

The boys knew their father meant every word. "I'm sorry, Daddy. I only pulled the tree. Donnie yanked it, and that's why it rolled faster," sobbed Lonnie.

"Nonetheless, you began the whole experiment, didn't you?"

"Yes, sir, I did."

"I'm sorry too, Daddy," Donnie sobbed. "I did give the rope a jerk. I won't ever do it again. I know now what my demise caused us."

Mr. Drake reached down and pulled Lonnie up from the bed where he was sitting quietly. Giving him a quick hug first, Mr. Drake then turned Lonnie over on his stomach in a crouched position with his hands tucked underneath his chest. Raising his hand in a primitive gesture of discipline, Mr. Drake slightly popped Lonnie on his behind.

The rest of the family members waited in silence to possibly hear what they couldn't see. The noises in the bedroom grew louder by the minute. They heard a loud slap and then another, and then the room returned to a quiet whisper. Once again, the family heard two loud slaps, and then silence filled the bedroom chamber again.

"Hey, what happened?" screamed a small, rapidly speaking voice from the telephone receiver. "Hello! Willie? Are you there? Did we get cut off?" Uncle Tom repeated over and over again through the dangling receiver that Willie immediately dropped during the bombardment. He had forgotten all about the phone call. In all the excitement, he dropped the receiver, and Uncle Tom was still engaged in a conversation of why he wasn't present for the holiday meal. "Would somebody talk to me?" Uncle Tom yelled.

"Oh, no!" exclaimed Willie. "I forgot about Tom. He's still on the line."

As Willie explained the whole incident to Tom, Mona and Mildred smiled at each other and almost burst out into contagious laughter. In order to constrain themselves from such rude behavior though, they knelt down to the floor and sniggered lowly as each one picked up broken ornament pieces that remained scattered over most of the hallway floor.

"Tom, I'm sorry," Willie explained, "the twins did it again. You know they always do something new every year. Well, this time they outdid themselves. They broke up our family tradition." Willie laughed as he watched Mona and Mildred pick up the mixture of blue and red colored glass. "Right now, though, they probably wish it were tomorrow already." Willie continued his conversation with Uncle Tom.

The rest of the family went back to their meal and finished stuffing their faces. A few went back for seconds and even thirds, while the remaining few approached the desserts with much delight.

As for the twins, Donnie and Lonnie, they deviously smiled at each other with a complete sigh of relief as they waited for their timeout to expire. They were somewhat content this time with their father's disciplinary actions because unknown to their parents, both boys had tucked a thick layer of soft bathroom tissue inside the seat of their pants. Each one figured, if the experiment went wrong, they would be ready for a truce. Therefore, punishment for Lonnie and Donnie was not quite so severe, except for the timeout. So far, they hadn't come up with a plan to outsmart their parents on that part of the discipline. However, Lonnie was still working on it.

CHAPTER 2

THE KIDNAPPING OF JOEY

The next morning arrived too soon for Mona. The sun filled Mona's bedroom with an outburst of warm, glowing rays giving her a lazy day feeling. Mona peeked her head out from underneath the bed covers just enough so she could see the time illuminating on the wall. It read "9:00 a.m."

"Ah, I still have an hour to sleep." She yawned and hibernated back underneath the ocean blue linen clothes. An hour that seemed like seconds passed by, and Mona's alarm clock rang out with an explosive song. Mona remained covered from head to toe, not wanting to budge an inch from her cozy bed. The song on the alarm clock was very annoying, so she reached over and slapped the button abruptly. "Just five more minutes, and I'll get up, stupid," she snapped an insult to her clock and then buried her head underneath the covers again. Mona punched the snooze button over and over again as she had done the previous morning, trying to get a few more minutes of sleep. Not long after the last snooze though, the alarm went off again, so she gradually turned over and squinted her olive-green eyes to focus in on the time illuminating from her clock face.

"Oh, no, I did it again!" she said as she quickly sprang to her feet. "It's eleven o'clock? You should have been up already!" Mona snapped at herself as she grabbed a blue sweatshirt, pulled it over her head, and rapidly thrust her arms through each sleeve hole. She grabbed a pair of her favorite broken-in jeans, plunged her left leg inside the left leg of the jeans, lost her balance, and fell over onto the bed.

"Let's do this again," she directed herself once more. Mona stood up, balanced her body upright, and lifted her right leg. She thrust her leg into the right jean leg hole and, with a quick zip and a snap, flew out the bedroom door like a disturbed wasp heading for its opponent.

After the scuttle from the bedroom, she made a mad dash to the next room, which happened to be the living room. Mona frantically began an all points search for her brown over-the-shoulder purse. Upon the coffee table, the last place she searched, laid her brown purse. She clutched the bag and opened it abruptly, forcing its contents out onto the couch. "Where are they?" she asked herself with a frustrated whisper. Mona turned toward the coffee table and spied a set of keys that appeared to be the likeness of the set she was frenetically trying to find. "Ah, there they are!" she said to herself with a glee of delight.

As Mona ran to the front door entrance, her eldest son, John, met her on the way. "Mom, looking for these?" he asked holding up a set of car keys.

"Huh?" Mona was puzzled. Mona looked down at the car keys she was clutching in her right fisted hand and then with her eyes questioned the ones John was holding. Observing the key chain that read, "Greatest Mom," Mona reached out and snatched the set out of John's hand and replaced it with the other set she picked up by mistake. John tossed them down on a nearby table.

"Mom, where are you going in such a hurry?"

"Huh, oh, I told you yesterday I have to make a quick stop at the mall, remember?"

"Oh, yeah. Can I tag along?"

"That's 'May I tag along,' and yes you may, but I'm not going to spend hours in that hot mall with all those people shoving and fighting with each other. I just need to make a quick dash in and out. It shouldn't take ten to fifteen minutes to get what I need."

"That's cool, Mom, but didn't you say the mall closes at noon today anyway?"

"Oh, yeah, what time is it? We better hurry."

"Mom, tell me again, why the mall is closing early. It makes more sense to me, financially thinking that is, to be open on one of the busiest days of the year."

"Yeah, well, you're right, and they normally would be open, but somehow they experienced some kind of flood damage due to busted water pipes or something like that, so they have to close for repairs."

"Well, that makes sense."

"John, why do you want to come along, anyway? I told you I'm just going to run in and out."

"I just want to get out of this house for a while, that's all."

"Why does that puzzle me?" she asked.

"I don't know, probably 'cause everything puzzles you," he said coyly.

Mona glared into John's baby blue eyes. "You're not telling me something. I can tell. You never want to get out of the house. What's up?"

"Nothing."

Mona thought for a moment and remembered. "Oh, you want to make sure we get the right rim for your bicycle."

John forgot about the bicycle rim, but he used it as an excuse to escape. "Oh, yeah, that's right."

"No, that's not it. I can tell."

"Okay, okay, I just need some freedom."

"Ah, that sounds like Grandma's name should've come up by now."

"Okay, you guessed it. It is because of Grandma. You know how she is. She won't let me talk on the phone. 'It's not good for a grown man to stay in a small room and talk for hours to someone he can't see, smell, or touch,'" he said in a high-pitched old lady's voice in an attempt to imitate his grandmother's voice. "Oh, and that's not all," he continued, "get this, the reason I can't go outside and talk to my friends whom I can see, smell, and touch is because 'Somebody might take off with you, honey,'" he said again in a high-pitched old lady's voice.

"Well, John," Mona chuckled, "she's afraid that a desperado might kidnap you."

"A what?"

"A criminal, bad guy, kidnapper, scum, you know. Anyway, she still can't forget the past. Her sister was kidnapped when they were about seven or eight years old. Grandma, being the oldest, assumed it was her fault."

"That's a lot of guilt to carry around. Did they ever find her?"

"No, and Grandma's not going to let it happen again. That's why she's so protective."

"Okay, Mom, I understand, but I'm not eight years old."

"Well, John, there again I'll have to bring up another story. At about age fifteen, Grandma's youngest brother, Tim, disappeared. No one knew what happened to him."

"Man, no wonder she's paranoid. Did they find him?"

"Not at first. He finally came home one day, claimed he went walking and decided to see how far he could go."

"If I did that, I would have been grounded until I finally got married."

"Well, you're right about that, but we've wasted enough time. Let's get out of here."

On the way out the door, a short blast of wind passed between John and Mona. "What was that?" asked Mona in surprise.

Mona and John looked at each other and announced in unison, "Joey!" They marched to the van with intrigue.

"Where do you think you are going, young man?" Mona asked Joey who was waiting at the passenger door.

"With you guys. Josh wants to stay with Gandma but not me. No way, Jo-ay. She's not yockin' me up in that house any yonga."

John laughed. Mona glanced over at her oldest son with an expression of accusation.

"What? I didn't say anything to him. He made that assumption all by himself," John snapped to his defense.

"Boys, look, Grandma means well. She's only trying to protect you because she loves you."

"Yeah," said John, "Grandma loves us to death. She might as well stuff us in her old red suitcase." He laughed. "You know, the one with the broken zipper that she had to tie up before she came to visit us last Christmas? Remember?"

"Oh, I memba." Joey laughed. "She yost some of her cose, and we had to go back and pick them up."

"Yeah, and an old man found a pair of her large white underwear draped on his attaché case. Remember when her bra got caught in the turntable too?" He laughed. Both boys laughed aloud.

"Don't you think you're being unfair?"

"Unfair?" said John.

"No way, Jo-ay," said Joey, "Gandma is smothewin' my bwanches."

John laughed. "Your branches? Where'd you hear that phrase, stupid?"

"I heard it on the te-uh-vision yast night, ape face. Sounds cooh, huh?"

"No, not really, cone head."

Joey protruded his short, fat, and well-rounded tongue and added an ugly face to follow. "Weh, I yiked it, monkey bwef," he smarted.

"Well, good for you, hoof head."

"Hosh—," he began to debate with a reply but was interrupted.

"*Boys!*" Mona demanded. "That's enough."

"I was gonna say hosh head, Mom."

"Sure you were, banana nose," John quickly made a last retort.

"See, Mom, you didn't say anything to King John," Joey snarled sarcastically.

"That's enough, both of you. Let's go! I want to get this trip over with in a hurry. I know how the mall gets on holidays." Mona unlocked the doors with her electronic keypad, and everyone stepped inside the minivan.

"You're not going to be in there that long, Mom," suggested John.

"Nonetheless, just that little bit of time is too much for me."

"How come we had Christmas dinner early this year anyway? Isn't it our family tradition to eat Christmas dinner on Christmas day?"

"Yes, John, you're right, but we were having a hard time getting the family together this year, so we changed the date. Anyway, the date doesn't matter, just as long as we spend time together."

"Yeah, that's true."

After all the questions were answered, no one had anything else good to say, so for ten solitary minutes of peaceful silence, Mona was able to sit back and enjoy the moving scenery rushing before her eyes. Just when she began to daydream though, her eldest son broke the silence with loud musical sounds.

"Silence is gone, Mama. We need some waves. That'll make your foot get happy so we can speed up this trip."

"Maybe so, but it'll also get me a speeding ticket. Turn that thing down."

"All right."

"Mom," Joey whimpered, "I need to go to the bafwoom bad."

"Oh, Joey, can't you hold it. We'll be there in less than five minutes."

"I've been ho'ding it. You better huwy up and think of something fast, or I'm gonna go on the ca' seat."

"John, check underneath the backseat and see if you can find the travel potty."

John reached underneath the last seat and found a semisquared object. He pulled it out and lifted the lid cautiously, took a deep breath, and closed the lid back down quickly.

"Mom, how long has it been since you cleaned this thing?"

"Since *I* cleaned it? If my memory serves me correctly, dear, it was your turn to clean it out."

"Me? Why do parents always blame their children when they forget to do something?"

"I am not blaming you. It was your turn to clean it out. You were the last one that used it. You know the rule. The last person that uses it empties it."

"I know that, but I don't use this thing. Only the little boys do."

Mona and Joey, at the same time, retorted John's negative statement, "Oh, yes, you do."

Joey looked at John and shook his head. "Yes, you do, John. You used it when we went on the church picnic."

"Oh, yeah, that time, because the bathroom was two hours away. Who can wait two hours, especially after all that tea I drank before we left the house?"

"Even so, John," Mona replied, "that was the last time it was ever used, remember?"

"Oh, yeah I forgot. Okay, everybody, hold your nose."

John opened the lid, and Joey jumped up, unzipped his pants, and quickly released the pressure that he was holding so tightly. He then sat back down with relief this time and buckled up his seat belt.

John, on the other hand, wishing he had cleaned the travel potty from the last trip, quickly closed the lid, grabbed a can of aerosol, and held down the nozzle until the van was completely filled with a thick invisible mist of car scent fumes.

"Don't you think that's enough." Mona coughed. "I don't know which smell is worse."

"I do," said Joey, "and it's not the spway or the potty."

"Oh, Joey." John frowned. "That's disgusting."

"I'm sa-we. Mom said to yet it out in the bafwoom. We', this is my bafwoom. What do you aspect me to do, swe' up and expwode?"

Joey's remark caused Mona and John to bellow out with laughter. Joey sat back and smiled assuredly that he had created a funny joke. Before long, familiar road signs sprang up on the right shoulder. Mona turned right and pulled into the parking lot. She circled around the parking lot several times to find the closest parking space near the shopping mall entrance.

"Mom, just park somewhere, already," John irritatingly expressed disappointment with his mother's indecisiveness.

Mona spied a female shopper exiting the mall entrance and followed the lady all the way to her parked car. After the red Honda pulled out, Mona drove into the empty space. The boys swung open their doors and hopped out excitedly. Mona wasn't quite so energetic. She sighed a big sigh. "Oh, well, come on, boys. Let's get this over with as quickly as we possibly can."

Inside, the mall was packed with adults of all sizes, ethnic groups, and ages. There were children walking and babies being pushed in strollers. Mona squeezed her way through the shoppers to get to the second floor. She purchased a wrapped package from the More Than Jewels store and directed the boys toward the exit.

"Mom," John asked, "what about my bicycle rim?"

"Oh, I did say we were going to buy that today, didn't I?"

"Yeah, but that's okay. I can wait."

"No, come on. Lead the way."

"Mom, yook at that yady," Joey yelled with a deafening outcry so his mom could hear between all the busy noises around them.

Mona turned around and looked in Joey's finger pointed directions. To her amazement, one of the female customers couldn't wait to relieve herself in a nearby bathroom, so she pulled down her blue lingerie and began urinating in a corner of Drucker's Department Store. She, apparently, tried to find a hidden area and forgot about the open display window in front of the store.

"Oh my," Mona gasped. "I definitely do not need anything in Drucker's today. Come on, boys, let's get that rim and go home. This is getting to be too much for me already."

"Mom!" Joey screamed.

"What now?" questioned Mona. John and Mona turned around to see what Joey was yelling about again, but he wasn't anywhere in sight.

"Where did your brother go off to?" asked Mona.

"I don't know. He was right there. Mom! Look to your right. That man has Joey by the hand, and he's moving awfully fast," John explained loudly as he pointed and began running in the same direction.

"Wait, John, wait for me!" she yelled. Mona pushed her way through the crowd and ran after John's lead. "Where is he, John?" Mona shouted.

John pointed in a northward direction and bellowed back, "He's in the black suit."

Mona scanned the hallway as she ran, but there wasn't a man in a black suit anywhere. Then she saw a man carrying a child and recognized Joey's bare head bobbing in the air. The man in the black suit stopped and quickly glanced toward his left shoulder as if he were looking for someone. When he discovered Mona close behind in mad pursuit, the man detoured behind a blue door. That quick glance gave Mona full view of his face. Knowing she would have to give a description of the kidnapper, she tried to keep his appearance fresh in her memory. Mona rushed toward the blue door and turned the doorknob. The door was locked, and there didn't seem to be any other way to get inside.

"Open up this door, you monster," Mona screamed as she pounded on the door. She kept beating on the blue door, but no one made a sound inside. Moping over to a nearby bench, Mona began to sob silently, and then tears began to flow. John approached the bench cautiously.

"Mom, what's wrong?" John questioned his mother's painful cries.

"John, I lost him. He's gone. My baby's gone," she cried. Mona pointed at a set of three blue doors and cried out, "He's behind that middle blue door. I saw the man take him inside and shut the door."

"Mom, I saw him disappear inside that door also. There's nowhere else for him to go. If both of us saw him go behind that blue door, then we'll just wait until he decides to come out." John thought a minute. "Wait a minute, all we have to do is call the police. They'll get the door open as soon as they get here." John felt around inside his pants pockets in search of his cell phone.

"That's good thinking, John."

"Mom, you didn't happen to bring your phone with you, did you?"

"No," she continued crying, "I...left it in the car."

"So did I. Okay, don't worry," he said looking around. "There's a pay phone over there. We'll get that door open. Wait here and keep watching the door while I call the police," John reassured his mother. He walked toward the telephone that was only a few feet away, picked up the receiver, punched in 911, and explained his dilemma to the operator. The operator connected him to the police department. John explained the situation to Officer Crump, who happened to pick up the line. Officer Crump assured him a unit would be sent out right away. John hung up the phone and thought a moment.

"Willie, I could call Uncle Willie. He'll know what to do." John knew Willie would know how to handle the situation and help his mother at the same time, so he picked up the receiver again and, after compensating the telephone company for their service, dialed his uncle's number.

"Hello," Willie answered.

"Uncle Willie, we can't find Joey."

"What? Where did he go?"

"While we were shopping at the mall, someone grabbed him. We tried to keep up with him, but he got away. Willie, you have to come up here—hurry—Mom's not holding it together."

"Okay, John, but call the police after you hang up."

"I did that already, Willie."

"Okay, hang tight, I'm on my way."

John ended his quick conversation with Willie. Then pacing his walk back to the bench where his mother was sitting, he kept thinking, "It's my fault. I wished he would run away. We would have been gone, if I hadn't reminded Mom about that *stupid* bicycle rim." John grabbed his upper lip with his left hand attempting to control his grief, but the tears gushed down his face anyway. Wiping his eyes roughly with the sleeve of his jacket, so his mother wouldn't see that he was crying, John tried to be strong for his mother, until Willie arrived. When he reached the bench, Mona was still staring at the blue doors without looking away even once.

"Mom, I called the police, and they'll be here soon. I'm sure they'll find Joey. Don't worry, okay?"

Mona shook her head in a positive note and continued crying. "He was right behind me. Why didn't I hold onto his little hand?"

"Mom, you did the best you could. You didn't do anything wrong."

"No, John, I know how the mall gets this time of the season. I should've held onto his hand. John, call Willie for me, please."

"I already did, mom. He's on his way."

"Thanks, sweetie. I don't know what I would do without you. You're always there to help me when I need you."

John began to feel guilt, again. "Mom, I'm sorry. This is all my fault," John cried.

"How could this be your fault?"

"Remember when Joey and I argued yesterday, and I wished he would run away?"

"Oh, honey, just because you were angry and wished him away didn't cause it to actually happen. That's not possible. Don't ever think this is your fault. Children are taken every day. If it's anybody's fault, it's mine. I'm always so careful. Why didn't I hold onto his hand? I never thought it would happen to one of my children because I am so cautious. But it's not your fault, okay?"

"Sure, Mom, but I still feel responsible," John reluctantly agreed. Mona and John sat back and stared at the blue door. People walking by would turn and look too. One of the mall patrons asked if a movie star was waiting to come out from behind one of the doors. Another one asked if the janitor was all right. There were other stupid questions from time to time. Soon John and Mona switched from tears to laughter, but Mona remembered why she was there and began crying all over again.

"John, what if I can't remember the man's face. I tried to keep it fresh on my mind, but I'm just not sure now."

"Mom, don't worry, we'll get Joey back. I promise you." John hugged his mother. Even during John's embrace, Mona wouldn't take her eyes off the blue door.

Within a matter of minutes, the police were on the scene. John explained the whole story. "We chased the kidnaper to those blue doors," was the end of his story.

"Ma'am, did you get a good look at his face? Ma'am?" questioned Officer Mender.

John looked at his mom and tried to smile. Mona looked up at the police officer with one eye on the middle blue door. "Yes," she cried.

"Can either of you give me a description?"

"Yes, sir, I can," said John knowing his mother was still too upset to talk. "He was five feet, six inches, very thin profile, Spanish male, and he looked like he hadn't shaved in a week."

"Did you notice what he was wearing?"

"No," Mona whispered with a painful sob. She couldn't remember his clothes. She only remembered his face.

John glanced at Mona and then looked up at the police officer. "I saw his clothes, Officer. He was wearing a black suit with tiny gray pinstripes."

"Son," expressed Officer Mender, "that was a very good description. Are you planning on being a detective someday?"

"Thank you, but no, sir. I'm going to be a child psychologist."

"Ma'am, do you have a picture of your son?"

"John," she cried, "look in my purse." Mona finally managed to speak still staring at the blue door as she handed John her purse.

"Ma'am, are you okay?" asked Officer Mender.

John stopped searching for Joey's picture and looked up at the police officer. "She's watching the middle blue door, sir. She won't stop until someone opens it. We have no doubt that my brother is in there."

"Ma'am, the police officers are handling the situation right now. We'll get those doors unlocked, and if your son is in there, we'll get him out."

"*If?* There is no if, Officer! He *is* in there," Mona spoke to the officer boldly. Her nerves were on edge making her short tempered and moody. "If you'll just open that middle stupid door, you'll find him in there. I saw him go in there, and my son, John, saw the man take him in there also," Mona snapped quickly as she was getting restless waiting for someone to open the blue door.

John continued searching for a picture of Joey and found a recent photo of all three of the boys together on the playground. "Here, Officer Mender," John announced as he handed the officer a 3×5 picture, "Joey's the one on the right wearing the blue T-shirt."

"What was he wearing today?"

John looked at Mona still staring toward the blue door. She didn't say a word. "He was wearing blue jean pants, that same blue T-shirt in the picture I just gave you, and a blue jean jacket."

"Very good, son. How tall is your brother?"

"He's about three feet and five inches. I'm not real sure about the exact height."

"That's close enough. What about his weight?"

"Hmm, I don't know. I guess fifty or fifty-five pounds."

"Forty-five pounds," Mona interrupted.

"All right," the officer motioned for John to step away from Mona for a quick discussion.

"Son, you need to take your mother home. She doesn't look well."

"She won't leave, sir, not until someone opens that middle door."

"I understand, but if your brother is not behind one of those doors, your mother might not be able to handle the shock. I know what I'm talking about. I've seen this happen plenty of times. Is there someone like your father or a relative who can persuade her to go home?"

"My father passed away a year ago, but maybe Uncle Willie can help. That's my mom's brother. They're pretty close."

"Would you call him and get him down here?"

"Oh, I already did, sir. He's on his way."

"Good deal, son. Let me know when he gets here. Meanwhile, go on back and take care of your mother. I think we have all we need right now. If we need anything else, I'll let you know."

"Okay, thanks."

"Oh, and, son, you're doing a great job helping your mother. You took charge and didn't give up under pressure. I just thought you should know that."

"Thanks."

The police officer walked away and began conversing with other officers in the hallway. He showed the officers the photo of Joey and pointed over to the blue doors and then walked away.

John walked back to the bench and sat down by his mother. "What did he say, John?" she asked.

"Oh, nothing really. They're waiting for someone to get the key and unlock the doors. He wanted me to take you home though. Are you okay?"

"I'm okay. I just need to look behind that middle blue door. When I can see what's behind that one door, I can go home. You know that, John. You know you have to see behind it too, don't you?"

"Yes, I do, but, Mom, how are you going to handle the situation if Joey is not in there?"

"He is in there!" Mona became irritated as she pointed toward the blue door. "Why won't anyone believe me?"

"Mom, I believe you. I saw it too, remember, but what if the kidnaper had a trap door or something? Could you handle not seeing Joey, when they open those doors?" About that time, John spied Willie approaching the bench.

"Mom, it's Uncle Willie."

"Willie," Mona cried, and for the first time, she took her eyes off the blue door. Only for a moment though because after she and Willie hugged, Mona sat back down and returned to staring at the door again as if it were her job.

"Willie," John interrupted, "that officer wanted to talk to you."

"Me? Why?"

"I don't know. He just said let him know when you get here."

"I know what he wants," Mona complained. "He wants to get rid of me. He's been trying to send me home, but I'm not going anywhere, Willie. You tell him that. I won't leave here until I get to look behind that middle blue door."

"Let me talk to him and see what he wants." Willie left the bench where Mona was sitting and marched up to a group of officers.

"Officer Mender?" he approached one of the officers with a questionable name.

"Oh, Sergeant Mender is over there," one of the officers explained pointing backward.

"Thank you," he said. Facing the same direction as the officer's pointed finger, Willie treaded toward another group of police officers.

"Officer Mender?"

"Yeah, that's me."

"I was told you wanted to talk to me."

"You must be Uncle Willie?"

"The one and only."

"Well, I believe you could help us out a lot, if you would persuade your sister to go home. She doesn't need to be here when we open those doors. If the boy is in there, we don't know what condition he may be in. If he's not in there, it could be too severe for your sister to handle right now. I've been through this type of situation many times. Mothers just can't handle the trauma of a lost child well at all. Your sister is already devastated and possibly in a state of shock. You can tell that just by looking into her eyes. One more incident, and she could snap."

"Snap?"

"Comatose."

"Wow, I didn't realize it would be that severe."

"It happens almost every time. They pass out, are rushed to the ER, and stay in the hospital for days on end. Sometimes they snap back, sometimes they don't."

"Okay, Officer Mender, I'll see what I can do. She's a very stubborn, persistent woman though. If she has her heart set on something, she won't budge until she gets it, especially when it comes to one of her kids."

"I understand. Just try whatever works."

Before Willie parted company with the officer, a large man in a gray flannel suit with black pinstripes approached Officer Mender and announced, "They stay locked, officer. No one can get through any of those doors without a key."

"Nonetheless, sir, we want everyone of those doors opened right now," Officer Mender demanded.

"Okay, but you're just wasting your time."

"Just do it, mister. You see that woman sitting on the bench over there?" he asked pointing in Mona's direction.

"Yeah."

"She's the boy's mother, and she won't leave here until she sees that her son is not behind those blue doors."

"Okay, okay, I'll unlock the doors, but I'm telling you it's a waste of time. Like I said earlier these doors remain locked at all times." The man in the gray flannel suit fiddled with a large set of keys that were attached on a looped key ring. He fumbled through the keys to find the right ones.

"I don't see the key to the middle door, but the first door key is on this set."

"All right, don't just stand there, unlock it," hastily commanded Officer Mender.

The man opened the first blue door on the right and backed away for the officers to enter inside. Two officers stood on the right with their guns held shoulder height and pointed straight forward. Two other officers stood on the left of the door in the same position. They searched everywhere inside, but no one was found.

Mona watched intensely. "Willie, they're opening the wrong door. He went into that middle blue door. He didn't go inside the other two."

"Okay, Mona, just be patient for a minute. They're going to open all the doors."

"Okay, now open the second door," Officer Mender commanded.

The man fiddled with the large set of keys again until he found the key that opened the blue door on the left. Again, no one was found inside. The middle blue door was the only door left. Willie gripped Mona's hand. He was afraid for her to see a lifeless body.

The man in the gray suit pushed the key inside the keyhole and turned the lock, but the door wouldn't open. "Officer," he called to Officer Mender, "I'm afraid I can't get this one open."

"Why not?" questioned the sergeant.

"This key doesn't seem to be working. If memory serves me correctly, the janitor's key broke off into the keyhole, so I gave him the only key left on my key ring."

"Is there another key?"

"Well, no, because the janitor now has the master key. He's supposed to make a duplicate and return the master key back to me when he comes to work today."

"Call him. Get him over here, and get this door open."

"I don't know if I can do that, Officer. He doesn't come to work until five o'clock tonight. He's probably asleep right now. Besides, it's just a utility closet. There's no way out and no way in without a key. Again, you're just wasting your time."

Mona jumped up from the bench and swiftly rushed over to the man in the gray suit. "Listen, you stupid little man," she commanded him loudly, "you get that janitor over here and unlock this door right now. I don't care what you think. I know my son is in that closet."

"Look, lady," the man said, "the janitor works all night and sleeps during the day. I don't want to wake him up over something minor like opening this utility closet."

"Minor!" Mona flared up. "My child is missing! That's not something minor."

"I'm sorry, ma'am. I didn't mean that was minor. I meant the blue doors because they're only utility closets. No one can get in without a key."

"Well, the kidnaper did, because I saw him go through that very door that you say is locked!"

"You couldn't have, ma'am. Maybe you thought you saw him go through one of those doors, but they can't be opened without a key. I don't want to disturb our janitor when I know the kidnaper is not in there."

Mona's anxiety began to build higher. She reached over to the man, grabbed his slender arm, and spat furiously, "Look, Horse Head, you get the janitor over here right now, or I'll break the door down myself, and you won't need a stupid key!"

"Stupid little man? Horse Head?" Willie turned to John and whispered, "Did you and Joey have a disagreement lately?"

"Kinda."

Officer Mender raised his eyebrows, and his eyes seemed to have almost popped out of their sockets. The other officers that were chatting among themselves dispensed with their conversations and moved in closer to hear. They smiled with their heads lowered trying not to be noticed.

The man in the gray suit pushed Mona's hand away and snarled, "There's no need to get violent, Lady. I'll call the janitor."

"You bet you will, Jerk!" Mona snarled repulsively.

The man in the gray suit turned to Officer Mender and commented sternly, "Officer Mender, I assure you, if this woman damages any one of those doors, I will press charges."

"Go ahead, Shrimp Toes," Mona yelled, "press on. Those stupid, precious doors of yours can be replaced. My son cannot!"

"Just get the keys," he commanded sternly, "I'll take care of your worthless doors."

"Uh, son," Officer Mender called John over, "why don't you take your mother over to the bench and try to calm her down."

"Yes, sir."

"Willie," called Officer Mender motioning him to move toward him.

"Yeah."

Officer Mender placed his hand on Willie's shoulder and began walking off at a distance away from Mona. "Does your sister have any other children at home?"

"Yeah, one, why?"

"Maybe if you try reasoning with her. Tell her…what's his name?"

"Josh."

"Tell her Josh needs her right now."

"I don't know. She's really set on opening that door."

"I understand, but that man can have her arrested, if she gets violent. You don't want to see your sister go to jail, do you?"

"No, I don't, but what do I tell her about the door."

"Tell her, no, I'll tell her myself. What's her name?"

"Mona."

"All right. Talk to her, calm her down, and I'll be there in a minute. Oh, one more thing. Bring her down to the Main Street Police Station when she feels better tomorrow. We need to complete a full report with her present."

"Okay, I'll do that. Thanks!"

About that time, the man in the gray flannel suit returned, and Willie overheard him talking to the officer. "I'm still trying to reach the janitor. He's not answering the phone. I told you he sleeps during the day hours. I'll keep trying though."

"Fine, but just to let you know, if you don't get him here within half an hour, I'll bust that blue door down myself. Do you understand?" exclaimed Officer Mender.

"Your captain will hear about this."

"Go ahead. Call him. I'll even provide the number for you. When it comes to missing children, I'm sure he feels the same way I do."

"Fine. Don't do anything yet. I'm sure I'll get in touch with him soon."

"It's your door."

The man walked away infuriated. He yanked his cellular phone out of his pocket and began making calls.

Willie walked over to Mona and put his arms around her. "Mona," he said calmly trying to overcome Mona's anger and stubborn will, "you've got to let go, honey. Let me take you home. The police will call us when they know something. The janitor may not get here for hours. They haven't been able to reach him yet. Staying here won't get that door open, and it's only stressing you out."

"No, Willie," she began to cry, "I need to see behind that door. I have to make sure my baby isn't in there. I have to know."

"I know you do, but you're stressed out, and that man could have you arrested. Do you want to go to jail and not be able to hold your son when they find him?

"No, but I'm afraid if I leave, so will everyone else," Mona sobbed.

Officer Mender overheard Mona's last statement as he walked over, seized a handkerchief from his pocket, placed it into her hands, and sat down beside her. Willie excused himself and walked over to John to give the officer some privacy. Officer Mender placed his right arm around Mona and held her left hand in his left hand. "Mona, dear, I promise you no one is leaving this spot until that last door has been opened and thoroughly inspected inside. You have my word on it. I know what it feels like to lose someone you love. It's been a year since I lost my wife and my son in a car wreck. Every bone in my son's body was broken, and his little body was so badly bruised beyond recognition that there was absolutely no way he would have been able to survive. My wife's heart stopped beating, but they couldn't revive her. At least I know she didn't suffer. However, knowing the severity of all their injuries, I still waited at the hospital for long hours hoping they would live, but they didn't."

Mona cried and looked up into the officer's baby blue eyes. He had some small tears forming. "I'm sorry, Officer…"

"Bob."

"Bob. I'm being selfish, I guess," she said as tears began to flow.

"No, Mona, you're not being selfish. You're just being protective. Being an officer, I thought I could protect my family from everything, but I couldn't," he said and, he tightly embraced her into his muscular arms. Mona seemed to have melted into his embrace, and a sense of peace came over her.

Willie's eyes beamed a surprise as did the other officers that were watching. "Hey, what's with the Sarge?" an officer asked.

"Looks like he's in love," commented one of the officers. Other comments were tossed around. Then the officers quietly laughed.

"Mona, do you have any other children?" asked Sgt. Mender.

"Yes, I have three sons. You met John. He's my oldest and I have a younger one. His name is Josh."

"Where is Josh?"

"Oh, he's with my mother. The older boys wanted to go with me to the mall, but Josh wanted to stay with his grandmother."

"That's great. He's there with your mother safe, but he needs a mother, too, right? You can't just take care of Joey, and leave the other two out of the family picture. Am I right?"

"Okay, Bob, you've convinced me. I'll go home. For some reason, I trust you." Officer Mender turned sideways on the bench, but before he arose, Mona added a warning. "But, Bob, you better keep your word."

Officer Mender turned back around making eye contact with Mona and softly placed his left palm on the right side of Mona's face and his left arm was still wrapped around Mona's shoulder. He leaned over and whispered in her right ear. "You can trust me," he whispered. Calmness melted away Mona's fear.

"I don't know why," she said, "but I do." He smiled and slowly withdrew his hand from Mona's face and then calmly got up and walked away.

Mona turned toward her brother and said, "Willie, I'm ready to go home now."

Willie was shocked. "He's good," he said to John.

Willie grabbed Mona's arm, and John grabbed the other. They both escorted Mona down the corridor and stepped onto the escalator. Mona looked back at the blue doors for the last time. Her heart was pounding with fear, and tears streamed down her cheeks. Officer Mender smiled and waved good-bye to Mona. Mona tried to smile but couldn't.

After Mona was out of sight, Officer Mender yelled to another officer, "Let's get this door open now. Take it off the hinges, if we have to."

"Yes, sir," they all agreed.

"The rest of you men help guard the other entrances. We don't need all of you here." Two men stayed behind to guard the last blue door while the other officers left to other stations. Officer Mender stayed behind as well to keep a promise.

Willie and John walked Mona slowly through the parking lot. Mona cried all the way to the van. When they reached her forest green minivan, Mona stopped abruptly.

"Willie," she said, "I can't."

"Now, Mona, you agreed."

"No, that's not it. I can't drive the van home. If Joey escapes, he won't know where to go. If he sees my minivan, he'll know I didn't desert him."

"Okay, Mona, we'll take my car. John can pick up the van later."

They walked away from the minivan and headed directly for Willie's Grand Am. His car was parked farther away than he realized, but they finally reached it and drove off toward the exit.

In the meantime, the janitor arrived with a belt loop full of keys dangling down on his right side. He jangled the keys around until he found the one that unlocked the blue door utility closet number 2, which is what read on the label that was attached to one of the keys.

"We're sorry we had to call you in so early, mister," Officer Mender explained.

"Hooper's my name. You didn't bother me none. I came as soon as you called. I've been home all day just watching TV."

"You've been home all day watching TV, not asleep?"

"That's right, why?"

"Well, your supervisor said he couldn't reach you."

"My phone only rang once, and I came out as soon as I heard. That poor lady. I hope she finds her baby. I don't see how he could be in here though," the janitor continued talking while he unlocked the door. "There you are."

Two officers approached the door with their guns held high in the air. The closet was thoroughly searched, but no one was found inside.

"Nothing here, continue your search," Officer Mender announced into a walky-talky.

"Copy. 10-4," voiced an answer from the speaker.

The officers left the area, and the hallway was bare, except for one soul. The man in the gray flannel suit returned to the hallway. He was talking into a cellular phone, saying, "It's too risky. You'll have to take him with you this time. When I knock on the door three times, you'll know it's safe to come out. Take the boy to your house, and I'll contact you there."

"I don't like this. Hurry up!"

The man in the gray suit walked by the blue door, pounded three times with his fist, and then briskly walked away.

Inside the closet concealed behind a hidden compartment, silently rested a slender man. When the three bangs upon the door were heard, he escaped from his secret compartment, climbed onto a ladder, and opened the ceiling tiles. The desperado carefully lowered the lifeless child he had hidden in the ceiling and laid him down on the floor. He pulled a clothes hamper out of the closet and laid the child inside. Then he covered his motionless body with rags and other pieces of material he found. The kidnaper redressed his attire from suit to a pale blue janitor's uniform shirt and jeans. Cautiously, he peeked around the corner of the door and exited with the hamper.

Pushing the hamper out the side exit door, the kidnaper swiftly headed toward an old brown Chevy station wagon. The man opened the hatchback to his Chevy station wagon, lifted Joey out of the hamper, and rapidly placed him onto the blue-carpeted floor. He then covered his seemingly lifeless body with an oblong box that was postmarked for mail service. Confidently, the desperado hopped into his wagon and headed toward the mall exit.

CHAPTER 3

THE EXIT CHASE

The traffic was backed up for a few blocks since the mall doors were closing and policemen were checking every car. Willie, Mona, and John had a very long wait, before they could exit from the mall. No one spoke. They just sat in silence and waited.

Even though waiting was uncomfortable for Mona and her family, it put a damper in the kidnaper's plans. A quick response from the police department prolonged his immediate getaway because he had to wait in a long line with just one way out of the mall. All the other exits were blocked off, and every car was being searched. When the kidnapper approached the exit for his turn to be investigated, a policeman looked inside his car for other passengers.

"What's in the box?" he asked.

"Oh, a present for my niece in Chicago. I'm sending it out in the mail today. It won't get there for Christmas, but at least she'll get it," answered the kidnaper trying to talk his way through the exit. "It's one of those large talking bears. Have you seen them? You can…"

"Yeah, I know what you're talking about. Okay, you can go," said the officer and flagged him through.

Willie pulled up behind the brown station wagon that had just been flagged through. The officer looked inside and flagged Willie through as well. Willie flashed his left blinker and turned in the same direction the brown station wagon happened to be going.

Underneath the oblong box, the small child began awakening from his dose of sleep aids. The drugs were beginning to wear off a little sooner than normal compared to most of the children the kidnaper was use to stealing. For Joey, though, he always had a large tolerance for medications. Although, still a small amount of drowsiness, Joey was able to quietly crawl out from underneath the box that once covered his motionless body. He peeked out the back window of the wagon and noticed some friendly, familiar faces. His little eyes lit up with happiness as tears rolled down his puffy cheeks. The distraught child began to wave and smile frantically to get their attention, but they seemed to be having a deep discussion, and no one noticed Joey at first.

John, on the other hand, was in deep thought gazing silently out his side window as flashbacks appeared in his mind. He couldn't forget a conversation he had between himself and two of his classmates. They insisted that whatever you wished for and if you wished hard enough, it would truly happen. John remembered what he wished for and began to form tears in his eyes. He wished for a second chance. *God, please, give me a second chance. I'm sorry I wished for my little brother to disappear. I honestly didn't mean it*, he thought to himself as he continued to remember the past events. About that time, he glanced up a moment and noticed his little brother waving from the back of the station wagon right in front of them.

"Mom! Willie!" he yelled.

"What?" they yelled back in unison.

"Look," he yelled pointing, "it's Joey!"

"Who?" asked Willie.

"What? Where?" questioned Mona.

"There. In front of us in that station wagon."

Mona and Willie looked toward the back window of the car in front of them, and Mona screamed, "Joey, it's my baby. Willie, look, it's Joey." Mona began waving back at her son; then, the others began waving back at Joey also.

"What are we going to do, Willie? If we go back to the mall to get the police, we'll lose him again."

"We're not going back, Mona. We'll just have to keep following him and see where he stops."

"Willie, please don't lose that car."

"Don't worry, I won't."

After a few miles, the kidnaper noticed Joey was out of his box and waving at the car behind him. He recognized Mona's face and, in desperation, pushed on the gas pedal in order to escape.

"He saw us!" yelled Willie.

"Oh, no. Willie, stay close to him."

"Mona, sit back and be quiet. You're making me lose my concentration."

"John," Willie called, "write this down, quick!"

"Okay, wait a minute. I have to find a piece of paper."

"Hurry up!"

John bent down to the floorboard and picked up a piece of scrap paper. He searched for a writing utensil but couldn't find one.

"Mom, do you have something I can write with?" he panicked.

"Hold on. I'll check my purse."

"You two hurry up before he gets too far!"

"We're trying to, Willie," Mona exclaimed speedily pouring out the contents of her purse in search for a pen or a pencil.

"I found one!" Mona excitedly cheered. Mona pulled out a slender, pointed object and handed it over to John.

"An eyebrow pencil?" he flouted.

"It'll have to do, John," Willie scorned. "Write this down quickly. M...Y...6...3...5."

"M...Y...6...3...5," John mumbled.

"Got it?"

"Yeah, got it."

"Good, now write this down."

"I don't have much more room on this little piece of paper, Willie," John called back as he held up a half an inch piece of paper.

"Abbreviate," he exclaimed, paused, and then continued, "brown '75 station wagon, hatchback, white top, dent to left front fender, mudguards, tiger tail on rearview mirror." Willie paused again to think as he searched frantically for more descriptions. "Oh, and a cardboard box in the back. Got that?"

"Cardboard," he paused a moment, "box, got it."

"Oh, well, that's just great," Willie said disgustingly.

"I'm sorry. I wrote it down as fast as I could," said John defending himself.

"What's wrong, Willie?" Mona asked.

"Look behind us."

Mona turned around to see what was behind them and observed two flashing lights, one red and one blue. "It's the police! That's great!" exclaimed Mona.

"No, Mona, that's not great. We're the one that's being pulled over, get it."

"But why? What did we do?"

"In case you haven't noticed, Mona, we've been speeding."

"So we'll just explain to them why we're speeding. I'm sure all the police officers have heard about the kidnapping."

"Yeah, but this is not a regular police car. It's a highway patrol vehicle. They only patrol the highways. They won't know anything about the kidnapping."

Willie began slowing down and proceeded to pull the car over to the right shoulder of the freeway.

"Willie, you can't pull over now. We'll lose him!" Mona scolded and grabbed the steering wheel.

"Mona, I have to," Willie insisted.

"No!" Mona demanded and grabbed the steering wheel again making the car weave in an attempt to turn the car back to the pursuit.

"Mona, what are you doing? You're gonna get us killed," yelled Willie as he grabbed the wheel and pushed Mona out of the way. Willie pulled the car over to the shoulder, stopped, and waited for the policeman to approach his car. While he was waiting, Willie fished out his driver's license from his wallet and held it between his pointer and middle finger. He figured he could quickly retrieve the ticket and be on his way again.

A medium frame police officer with broad muscular shoulders approached the car and piercingly looked down at Willie. "Okay, Mac," he bellowed in a deep voice, "get out of the car."

Willie froze instantly. "He wants me to get out of the car, Mona. This is worse than I thought," Willie whispered trying to move, but his body remained immovable.

Mona reached over and poked him. "Willie," she whispered back to him, "I think he wants you to get out now."

"I know that, Mona, stop poking me. My body won't move," Willie complained and pushed at Mona's arm to shove it out of the way. Gradually lifting the door handle, he managed to open the door as his whole body trembled with fear. He stepped out of the car with both feet placed firmly on the ground.

"Turn around, face the car, and place your arms above your head," he commanded.

"Officer," he tried to explain politely, "I can explain. We were chasing that brown station wagon up ahead."

"Stalking were you?"

"Yeah, I mean, no. The driver of that vehicle kidnapped my nephew. That's why we were speeding…to keep up."

"Uh-huh," was all he said.

"You don't believe me, do you?"

"Uh-uh."

"Great."

"Honestly, Officer," Mona tried to explain poking her head through the driver's window, "my baby was in the back of that station wagon, and he was waving at us the whole time. That's why we were following the station wagon. Sir, no offense, but you need to do your job and go get my son back."

The officer looked over at Mona when she made her last comment and replied, "Look, lady, everyone has a good excuse for speeding, but I'll have to admit this one is a first."

"Okay, Mac, feet apart, hands behind your head."

"Sir," Willie panicked, "am I under arrest."

"You were speeding, swerving on the road, and failure to pull over. That's a criminal offense."

"But, sir, I was speeding because I was trying to keep up with the kidnaper. I was swerving because my sister was trying to make me stay on the road, and I didn't pull over because I was afraid we would lose track of the kidnaper's station wagon."

Mona noticed the handcuffs and shrieked, "Officer, what are you doing that for? Just give us a ticket and let us get the heck out of here."

"Well, ma'am, you see, as I told your husband…"

"Brother."

"As I told your brother, you weren't just speeding. Your car was weaving all over the road, and you failed to stop. That to me, ma'am, is a sign of reckless driving, possible drinking," he said as he continued searching Willie, clamped down the handcuffs, and pulled him away from the car. Willie glared down into the window and stared into Mona's olive-green eyes. For once in her life, Mona didn't have much to say. She was actually frightened.

"Officer," Willie tried to defend himself further, "no matter how bizarre it may sound to you, we're telling you the truth. If you'll check with Officer Mender at the Police Station on Main

Street, he can confirm the kidnapping that just happened about an hour ago at the mall."

"Okay, sir, I'll check out your story, but in the meantime, I'll have to bring you in the squad car down to the station. If your story checks out, you're free to go, but if not, I'll have to book you."

"Ma'am," the officer directed his conversation to Mona, "you can drive, can't you?"

"Yes, I can, little policeman. Why do you ask?" she snarled sarcastically.

He wasn't sure what to say next after her "little policeman" remark, so he continued to give her directions. "Follow me, please. Oh, and, little sister, the speed limit this time, okay?" he said in a teasing gesture.

Mona's fear dissipated instantly. Instead, she became infuriated with the officer. "Right, Mr. Officer, sir." Mona smarted with a grumble and sideways stuck out her tongue.

"I saw that," he remarked loud enough to be heard and slightly smiled where Mona couldn't see him.

Mona started the engine, turned toward the police officer, batted her eyes a few times as she popped out a fake smile, and then took off in a rush.

"You have a very feisty sister, sir," he said to Willie as he started his engine and took off after Mona.

"You have no idea. When she puts her mind to something, she doesn't let go easily."

"I can see that. Is she always like this?"

"Ever since I can remember. My parents couldn't believe a girl could be so mischievous, so I had to take the wrap for her when she got into trouble."

They both laughed.

"She's definitely mysterious, but in a cute way though," he remarked and sped up a little faster to catch up with Mona. After he approached the back of her bumper, he flashed his blinker and gave a jaunty smile as he passed in front of her vehicle.

Mona wasn't sure how to take his reaction, so she decided to toy with his attentiveness. She pulled her car over into the left lane, waved, smiled jauntily, and passed in front of the policeman's vehicle.

Willie couldn't believe what he was witnessing. His sister was flirting with the police officer, and he was enjoying it. Another thought approached his mind though. *Hmm*, he thought, *maybe I won't get a ticket after all.* Then Willie sat back and enjoyed the ride.

After Mona and Officer Murphy stopped flirting, Willie explicated the whole story in more detail. By that time, they had reached the station on Main Street, and the three speeders were escorted inside and told to sit in the waiting area. The arresting officer went inside one of the offices for about fifteen minutes and returned smiling. Officer Murphy discussed his regrets to Mona about the whole situation and directed Mona to the front office to fill out a statement about her missing child. He took the handcuffs off Willie's wrists and stated, "I contacted Officer Mender and told him everything. He's on his way back to the station to handle the investigation."

"Thank you," commented Willie. Officer Murphy turned and walked away.

Another officer walked up to Mona and expressed his regrets as well. He was calm and gentle. Mona liked his approach, so she continued talking to him for a long time.

"You're going to get your son back, Ms. Melnick," Officer Henson reassured her. "Don't worry, our precinct has a good record for finding lost or kidnapped children."

"Thanks, Officer Henson," she said reading his nametag. Officer Henson reached out to shake her hand. The handshake lasted longer than a normal two-second handshake, and their eyes were in close contact. Mona smiled, and Officer Henson smiled back. He then escorted her back to the waiting area.

"If you need anything or have any questions, ma'am, give me a call," Officer Henson spoke as he reached in his chest pocket to retrieve a business card. He then gave it to Mona, turned, and walked away.

Willie stared at Mona with bewilderment.

"What?" she asked.

"Ah, nothing, forget it," was all he said.

Another police officer walked into the waiting area and explained politely, "We have everything we need. You're all free to go home. We'll contact you when we get something concrete."

"What *are* you going to do, Officer Johnston?" questioned Mona as she looked down at his nametag.

"Well, ma'am, we'll bring in the driver of that brown station wagon for questioning. Great job on the description! The rest will depend on his statement and what evidence we can gather."

"Oh, that's just peachy," commented Mona with a sardonic reply. "We almost had him until Mr. Hoof Head in the big blue suit over there came in on the scene and stopped us for speeding." Mona raised her voice as she pointed toward the officer that arrested Willie for speeding. He was conversing with another officer a few feet down the hall and didn't hear Mona's remark.

"You mean Officer Murphy? Ma'am, he's a good officer. I'm sure he was only doing his job, and you know as well as I do, ma'am, that speeding and reckless driving is against the law."

Mona's face lit up like a flaming hot candle. "And kidnapping isn't?" she exploded, turned swiftly, and marched out the front door without another word spoken.

"I'm sorry," Willie apologized, "she's a little torn up right now."

"That's okay, sir, I was prewarned about your sister."

"Oh," he said with a little unsure chuckle, "well, thanks a lot," Willie said as he turned and rushed out the door in an attempt to catch up with his sister. John followed behind.

After Willie was out of sight, Officer Johnston yelled down the hallway to Officer Murphy, "Now, that's one mad mama!"

Officer Murphy and another officer walked over to where Officer Johnston was standing and laughed. "I told you to look out 'cause that one bites."

"That you did," he agreed, and they burst out with laughter.

"Kind of cute though, wouldn't you say, Al?" Officer Johnston looked over at Officer Murphy. Officer Murphy just smiled and raised his eyebrows in agreement.

Another officer jumped into the conversation and commented, "You should've been there when Officer Mender questioned the woman. He was quite taken with her also."

"Officer Mender? No way. He's not taken with anyone," reminded Officer Murphy.

"You sound a little jealous." Officer Johnston tried to tease.

"Jealous? Not a chance."

"All right, I'll bet you Officer Mender asks her out before you do?" Officer Johnston continued to tease.

"Who said I was going to ask her out?"

The group enlarged with more police officers after the conversation grew interesting. The group of officers began putting down wagers to bet on who was going to ask Mona out first. Officer Mender walked by, and the group called him over.

"Officer Mender, want in on our bet?" asks Officer Johnston.

"What bet?"

"Who's going to ask that spicy woman named Mona out first?"

"What? Ask her out? She's a client."

"Come on, Officer Mender. You know you like her."

Officer Mender smiled shortly and commented, "Well, she is kind of cute."

All the officers in the group began cheering. "Mender, Mender he's our man. He can get the girl when nobody else can," they chanted.

"All right, you're on. What's the bet?" asked Officer Mender.

"Between you and Murphy, which one can ask her out first and get her to agree on the date," Officer Johnston reiterated the bet in question.

"Okay, you're on," agreed Officer Mender.

"Murphy?" questioned Johnston.

"Yeah, sure, I'm in," Officer Murphy agreed.

Mona, Willie, and John walked out the front door of the police station and piled into the car. On the way home, Mona sat back quietly, but inside her conscious mind, she was scheming a plan. John turned to Willie and whispered, "She's up to something, Uncle Willie, look at her face. She's in another world."

Suddenly, the frown on Mona's face began to turn into a glowing devious smile. "I've got it," she plotted as the bright idea finally submerged, and the imagery of a lightbulb mirage merged above her head.

"Do you see what I see?" asked John.

"Yeah, but it's just our minds playing tricks on us," Willie commented about the lightbulb image.

"Hey, you two, listen," she raised her voice to get their attention.

"I'm afraid to ask, Mona. What now?"

"Never mind. You're not ready to hear this. I can tell."

"Mona, I don't like the look on your face. What do you have cooking in that mysterious brain of yours?"

"Oh, nothing. Don't worry, Willie, I've got everything under control. Trust me, everything's gonna be okay."

"Spill it, Mona. What do you have cooked up now? I mean, you got me arrested, what could be worse?"

"Okay," she began, "I just figured out how we can get Joey back."

"We? Did you say we?"

"Well, I obviously can't do it alone."

"Do what, Mona? Do what?" Willie asked.

"Listen carefully. After the police call the kidnapper in for questioning, we'll wait for him to leave the station. We can follow behind him and see where he goes and maybe he'll lead us straight to Joey."

"And what if he doesn't?" asked Willie.

"Well, that's when we'll have to take over. You know, take drastic measures."

"There's that word 'we' again."

"Well, Willie, it does take at least two people to make a we."

"Yes, I'm fully aware of that, but why does it always have to be me when you say the word 'we'?"

Mona smiled at Willie with a lost puppy dog expression. "Please, I can't do this alone."

"Mona, you are my sister. You can't get away with batting those green eyes of yours and expect me to follow in a trance like those police officers."

Mona sat back and began to cry. "If you don't help me, I'll never see my son again."

"Okay, Mona, what do you have in mind?"

"Yeah, Mom, what *do* you have in mind?" John asked intrigued.

"Well, we'll follow him to his house and question him. That's all."

"That's all! Mona, this man is a professional kidnaper and probably a killer too. We don't know anything about being detectives."

"Maybe so, Willie, but I think we can handle it, if we put our minds to it. You're pretty good with karate, and I think I've seen enough detective shows to get us inside the front door. I really think we can do this."

"Oh, man, Mona, you're going to get us killed. You have really lost it now."

"I may have lost it, Willie, but I'm getting it back, and it ain't getting out of my hands ever again. Next time, I will be prepared. No one will take one of my babies ever again," Mona continued to ramble for a while and then became silent.

"John, want to drive your mom's minivan home?"

"Sure, but didn't Mom want to leave it there in case Joey escaped."

"Yeah, but now we know he's not at the mall. I doubt if the kidnaper even goes back to the mall. Not with Joey anyway."

"Yeah, I guess you're right," agreed John.

Nothing more was said from anyone the rest of the way to the mall. John hopped out of the car, dashed into Mona's minivan, and began his cruise home. Willie followed his lead and listened to some relaxing contemporary music while Mona, still in her own private make-believe world, sat back quietly, and didn't make a sound. To Willie, Mona's stillness was a great blessing.

CHAPTER 4

THE SEARCH FOR JOEY

The ride home remained silent; not a word was uttered, except for soft music that Willie tuned into the radio. Willie stayed serene listening to his music, while Mona just stared out the window thinking about her missing child. She sobbed as she glanced back to the trauma that took away her son. "It's my fault." Mona sobbed silently. "I shouldn't have let him get so far away from me," she cried inside her wearied heart. "Right now, he could be crying for me, and I can't do anything about it." Large teardrops formed in her eyes and then gushed their way down her cheeks like a waterfall. "Oh, dear God, please protect my son from these desperadoes. Don't let them take my baby away from me. Please help me get him back." Mona's tears continued flowing until it seemed there was no more water left to cry. Suddenly, as if someone slapped her on the face, Mona's sobs changed course and turned into anger. "No," she demanded as she pictured thoughts in her head. "I refuse to let any lower-life scum force me to give up," she cried. "I'm not giving up," she said to herself as she dried away the remainder of the tears on her face. "I'm coming for you, baby. Your mama's coming to take you home where you belong," Mona promised. "No matter what it takes," she kept repeating, "no matter what it takes."

"Did you say something, Mona?"

"Huh, oh, no."

Mindfully, Mona began plotting courses of action to retrieve her missing son. So when they finally reached her driveway, Mona was pumped and ready to pursue her ruse. No one or not one thing was going to stand in her way.

Willie pulled into one of the empty spaces of Mona's three-car garage, turned off the motor, and slowly leaned against the car door to push it ajar. With a tired, grunting noise for each movement he made, Willie forced his entire body to a standing position and then proceeded to take a few tiny steps toward the kitchen door. Mona, on the other hand, dashed out vibrantly, as if she were on an important mission. She reached the kitchen threshold about the time Willie drudgingly managed his first two steps. She reached out to unlock the kitchen door but paused briefly to ponder upon her plans. Then Mona turned toward Willie and smiled at him as he moaned and groaned with his left hand pressed against his tired aching back.

"Willie, what are you moaning about?" she asked.

"Well, number one, I had to stand up the whole day at work yesterday; I know I must have walked twenty miles. And two, do you realize how long we've been driving in that car?" he complained.

"Okay, Willie, come on inside and take a break." She sympathized as she dashed inside the kitchen. "There's really nothing you need to do right at this minute anyway," Mona calmly commented as she stayed her mind on a bookshelf in the kitchen.

Mona frantically searched the bookshelf for specific books. While she searched, her mother walked in and asked, "Mona, where's Joey? I wanted to give him something."

"Oh, Mama, Joey was kidnapped at the mall."

"What? Oh, my," she said and sat down in one of the kitchen chairs.

"Mom, are you okay?"

"Mona, I tried to get him to stay here. He wanted to go with you."

"Mom, we're going to get him back. Willie and I have come up with a plan to find him and get him back."

"A plan? *You and Willie*? What are the police doing about it?"

"I don't know mom. I guess whatever they do in the case of a kidnapping, but I'm not going to wait for them. I have to do something."

"You're right. You do have to do something or it will make you crazy," she said and hugged her daughter. Mona tried not to cry, but tears rolled down her cheeks.

"Well, you and Willie go do your thing," Mona's mother suggested after the long hug ended.

Mona's mother noticed Josh had been listening, so she added, "Josh and me will find plenty of things to do, while you are gone. Right Josh?"

"Right, Grandma," Josh said as he was creeping into the kitchen. Josh overheard their conversation about his brother and his face saddened.

"Mom, are you going to bring my brother back to me?"

Mona looked into Josh's tearful eyes and assured him that Joey was going to be found, and then she gave him a hearty hug. "You stay here and guard the house and keep grandma safe, until we come back with your brother, okay?"

"Okay, momma," he said with tears running down his little cheeks, "I know you will."

"Come on Josh, let's leave your momma alone so she can think." Mona's mother grabbed Josh by the hand and they walked out of the kitchen talking and laughing. Mona's mother always knew how to brighten the sad days. She guessed it was because of all the bad times her mother experienced growing up.

"Where is that book?" she asked herself. "Oh, there it is." She joyfully observed and held up a book titled *How to Survive* and then grabbed another book called *Stakeouts*.

"Oh, no! You're thinking again, aren't you?" Willie said as he entered the kitchen. He seemed to have forgotten how tired he was and changed the channels of his mind. "That could be dangerous for me. I remember when we were children, you always came up with hair brain schemes from some book you read, and I was the one that always got into trouble, not you."

"Willie," she tried to interrupt.

"No! Whatever it is, Mona, the answer is no."

"Okay! I was just going to remind you of the time when Mama accused you for that fire in the backyard, and I told her you didn't do it."

"Yeah, I know. And you took the blame for me. I should've known you were going to bring that up again. How many times do I have to relive that moment? It was your idea that got me into trouble in the first place, you know, you and that science experiment book."

"I know that, so what if I never bring it up again."

"I don't get it. Where's the catch? As usual, what do *I* have to do?"

"Well, nothing really, but I do need a couple of tiny, little favors." Mona held up her hand with two fingers pinched tightly together to indicate a very small task was at hand.

"Do I even dare ask what those tiny favors might be?" he asked pinching his two right hand fingers together like Mona and then opening them as wide as he could get them to indicate the task was going to be bigger than Mona mimicked. The whole time Willie's face held a wild air of disbelief.

Mona smiled sadly and shrugged her shoulders without a single word. Silence was a dead giveaway for Willie. If Mona didn't speak, he was fixed in the plan already. He knew there was no way out.

"Fine, what do you want me to do? Plan a riot at the police station? Or maybe you want me to kill someone. You know, tiny, little favors like that?"

"Oh, be reasonable, Willie. What I need is very simple."

"Simple? I don't think so, Mona. You've never ever planned anything simple in your life. What do you want from me, Mona?"

"Okay. I just need you to get some guns and ammunition for our journey. That's all. Can you take care of that tiny, little favor for me, please?" she said pinching her fingers again.

"Simple? Tiny? You call that a tiny favor? Mona, what do you need guns and ammunition for anyway? What could you possibly be conspiring in that head of yours this time?"

"Willie, I've got a great plan to get Joey back, and I know it will work. Just trust me."

"You always say that, 'I know it will work. Trust me.' Then that's when I end up with the bad end of the deal. Usually, I get grounded or something similar," Willie continued to complain. "Wait a minute, you just said our journey, didn't you? Oh, no! We're not dealing with Mom and Dad this time. We're talking jail time. Big Bob's waiting to make me his male companion against my will at cellblock 5. I've got to get out of here before you make me turn into a criminal. I don't know what it is about you, Mona, but you can make me do things I don't even want to do. To top it off, if Mama hears about it, she'll turn me in and have me sent to prison for life 'cause you couldn't do anything like that."

"You're not going to prison, silly."

Mona turned completely around, met Willie face-to-face, and stared into his dark-blue eyes. Placing the palms of her hands on each side of his face, she solemnly spoke, "Willie, I can't do this alone, okay. I desperately need your help. Joey needs your help. He's counting on the both of us to bring him home safely. Willie, if we don't do something fast, they'll move him so many times we won't know where to begin searching. Time is precious. Okay?" she softly spoke with tears swelling up in her eyes.

One look into Mona's somber eyes was enough. Right then, she could have asked for anything, and Willie would have given it to her. "Oh, all right," he said tenderly as he was drawn into her web. Willie surrendered to Mona's hypnotic approach, but he added an ultimatum to show he wasn't giving up without a release. "But if I do this, Mona, you promise me you won't bring up that incident about the backyard ever again? And you won't ever tell Mama it was really my fault."

"Never again. Not a word."

"Fine, consider it done, and you better keep your word," Willie commented not really caring whether Mona mentioned the incident again. He just wanted to be somewhat in control.

"Trust me."

"Never." Willie grabbed his back and began to moan again. "Why didn't you tell me about this great idea of yours, before I got out of the car?"

"Oh, I don't know, Willie. Probably because it just popped into my head when I started to unlock the kitchen door, and the whole plan didn't come together until I read a paragraph in my survival book."

"Survival book. I should have known. You always get ideas when you read. You should have never learned how."

Willie struggled to walk back toward his car still moaning with every step. By the time he reached the door to his vehicle, Mona stepped up to the kitchen entrance and quickly rushed through a second request that suddenly popped into her head again. "Oh, uh, Willie, there's one more tiny, little favor I need to add," she said squinting her eyes and pinching her two fingers together again.

"What else?" Willie whined.

"Uh, it would help a lot if you would bring your little mail truck back too," she said and without waiting for an answer or a complaint, closed the kitchen door quickly.

"My little what?" asked Willie completely surprised. "Mona," he whined again, "we can't use my work truck." By the time Willie managed to utter one word, Mona had already shut the kitchen door.

"I'll probably be looking for another job come Monday morning," Willie mumbled as he opened the car door and literally threw his aching body into the vehicle. "Why do I let her do this to me? This is the same woman who got me arrested for drunk driving, and I don't even drink. This is the same woman who lied to me as a child telling me her mud pies were merely brown because they were chocolate flavored so I would eat one, which I did. I don't even like chocolate!" Willie griped and complained until he reached the driveway to his house.

"Oh, she makes me so mad," he commented his last complaint to himself. "If it wasn't for those kids, I'd..." Willie stopped whining as his thoughts rested on his little nephew, Joey. Mona was right though; time was too precious. Joey's time was running out. If he weren't found soon, they would probably never find him. "Who cares if I lose my job," he cried out to himself. "Joey's life is more important than my job." So he decided the best thing to do was go along with Mona, no matter how wild her schemes, and be there to help in case her ideas got out of hand. "Okay, self, let's do it," he said trying to motivate his first step. First item on the agenda was to gather all the guns and ammunition he could find. Being a gun collector made part of Mona's first request easy. *Do I use blanks or live ammunition?* he thought. "Ha! Do I even need to ask myself that question?" He scoffed. "That would be like hosing down the car with gasoline and then giving Mona a match." Considering the source, he decided to use blanks, instead of live bullets.

After collecting all the provisions, Willie drove back to Mona's house in his mail truck as she requested. Mona was on her way out the front door carrying a seemingly heavy cooler from the strained expression upon her face. She deposited the heavy cooler on the front lawn close to the edge of the driveway and returned back inside the house.

Knowing Mona's intentions on taking the cooler along, Willie pulled up to the edge of the driveway and began packing the heavy cooler inside the small-scale space available in the back of the mail truck. As he scoped out the remaining space, Mona was inside gathering other items for the trip. Among the provisions were blankets, a gallon of distilled water, and a small coffee pot with a DC connection. In a brown paper bag, she gathered some instant coffee packets, hot chocolate mixes, and tea bags. Other food items were added to the grocery bag, as well as Styrofoam cups, plates, and plastic utensils. With her arms overloaded with supplies, Mona managed to hurriedly move toward the mail truck. She deposited the brown grocery bag and the other items near the mail truck and then dashed back inside the house without being noticed.

Willie stepped backward out of the mail truck and continued backing away from the truck a few small steps at a time as he was quite overtaken with the compact arrangement he had made for the cooler. He was very proud of himself. Still admiring his organizational skills, he moved one step back too many and bumped into the remainder of Mona's commodities. Losing his balance, Willie fell rearward over the pile of supplies. His feet popped up high into the air, as if he were going to do a retrograded handstand.

"Mona!" Willie bellowed out a distress call with disgust in his shallow voice, "What's all this stuff for? We're not going camping! It's those books you're reading, isn't it? Stop reading. It's bad for the both of us."

Mona didn't hear Willie's crash or his voice of complaints; she was in such a busy rush reading and thinking of what to bring next. The only sounds she could hear were her own industrious thoughts. She did, however, make time to talk to her famished son who was making a few sandwiches in the kitchen.

"John, did you park the car inside the garage?"

"Yeah, why?"

"I don't have time to explain. Now go put on your Christmas present that Willie gave you and meet me outside," she commanded and in haste scurried to another room.

With his mouth full of food, John tried to speak. "What for?" he mumbled a few slightly understandable sounds.

"Survival!" she yelled back from her room.

"Huh," John said confused.

"Just do it, John. It might be useful later."

Obediently, John went to his room and put on the new bicycle outfit that Willie bought him for Christmas and protruded anxiously outside.

"I'm ready," he announced to Willie before he lunged his teeth into the second sandwich.

In his intent confusion of trying to pack the little mail truck with the extra supplies and make room for the passengers, Willie didn't notice John's uniform at first. But taking a brief glance toward John's direction made Willie take a second view that lasted longer than a second. "What are you wearing that thing for?" Willie asked John with a perplexed expression upon his wearied face.

"I'm dressed up and ready for action," he commented with a big smile on his face.

"Oh, no you're not. Your mother is out of her mind right now. It's going to take a lot for me just to look after her with those crazy half-witted schemes she comes up with. I certainly do not need the son of a crazy woman to have to care for as well."

John quickly changed his jaunty attitude and began pleading, "But, Uncle Willie, please reconsider. You said it yourself, 'Mom's out of her mind.' Don't you think you could use some help with all that she's going to convince you to do? You know she's not finished with you yet. You know you're gonna need my help 'cause I can change her mind a lot better than you can. Come on, Willie,

I promise I won't get in the way." John pleaded and begged until Willie finally gave in to his persistence.

"Oh, maybe you're right. There's no telling what she's going to dream up next. I've been down that road way too many times. You should hear some of the hair brain things she made me do when we were kids."

"I have, Uncle Willie."

"All right, I guess you can go."

"Yes!" John pounced with excitement, "That's a big GTC for me."

"AGT what?"

"GTC. It means good 'til canceled. I found it in the dictionary during my English class. We had to look up ten unusual words or phrases and make sentences with them."

"You mean GTC is actually in the dictionary?"

"Yeah, pretty good, huh?"

"Interesting. Now, tell me what possessed you to put on that bicycle uniform?"

"Survival." Before John could finish explaining the reason behind his apparel selection, Mona pushed open the storm door with such great force it slammed against the side of the wall creating a loud bang. When she stepped out onto the doorsteps of the front porch in plain sight, the sunlight gleamed bright on her copper penny hair. Both Willie's and John's mouths dropped open so wide it appeared they were practicing for a doctor's visit. Their faces showered expressions of severe shock and surprise.

"Man," expressed John, "that's one mad mama!"

"Yeah," gasped Willie, "and she's really ready for survival.

"GTC on that."

"For sure."

Mona walked out on the lawn to announce her new wardrobe collection. The daylight showered her slender body and lit up the green military ensemble she was wearing. From head to toe, Mona was decked in military affair—masked with a beret, bandanna, boots, and enough artillery to blow the neighborhood block away, if it were loaded. She approached the mail truck with dignity and pride.

"To think it was supposed to be a gag gift," John remarked softly.

"Yeah," Willie agreed, "some joke."

"Well, I couldn't just throw it into my closet and not make some good use for it," Mona explained as she approached them.

"Mona, are we attending a costume party? First John, now you."

"No, I decided I need to feel and look the part of a vigilante for motivation," she said patting her bad artillery that was strapped around her waist.

Willie gasped, still in shock. "Mona, those guns are blanks and the grenades you have attached to you are hollow—pineapple duds, get it? Not to mention the other guns you have, which are toys you found in the playroom."

"Oh, I know that, but you can't tell the difference, can you? They actually look real!" she rejoiced.

"Maybe you or I can't tell the difference, but a professional killer knows. Did you think you were going to bluff your way with these people, Mona, with toy guns? Mona, they don't have a conscience. They'll kill you like you kill cockroaches and flies."

"I know that, Willie, but even professionals make mistakes sometimes. Nobody's perfect."

"Yeah, and you expect them to make that blunder when you walk in."

"I don't know, yeah, maybe," Mona shrugged. "Anything's possible. Anyway, I have my handy survival books to help me get through the tough spots," she explained as she held up five books on survival.

"Right. Mona, those books are for people who need to know how to survive in wartimes," he paused a moment and looked over at John expecting help. John shrugged his shoulders not knowing what was expected of him. "You're not bringing the books."

"What? No, Willie, this is wartime. We must fight to get Joey back, and besides, these books have great ideas."

"You're so hardheaded. You just won't listen. Those great ideas are gonna put you under the earth," he mumbled disgustingly.

"Some great help you are," he whispered to John.

"What? They're just books. Let her take the books."

"Fine, take the books," he mumbled.

"Oh, by the way, Mona, John is going along with us, and that's final, end of discussion, so don't try to change my mind," he demanded acting like a megaman with lots of control over dominate women.

Mona winked at John and in a sweet, gentle voice sighed. "Well, okay, Willie, if you insist." Then she opened the passenger door to the truck and stepped one foot inside. Willie stopped her before she entered the rest of the way.

"You're not wearing those guns in public," he demanded grabbing her right arm, still feeling in control.

"Okay, if it will make you feel better, I'll take them off for now, but I get them back." She gave in and took off all the hardware.

"Everybody in?" Willie asked.

"Yep," replied Mona and John in unison.

"Well, let's move on, Mad Mama." Willie backed the truck onto the road and stopped. "Mona, you haven't actually told me where we are going. Or do I need to wait while you read your book for more ideas?"

John laughed.

"No, Willie, I know where we're going."

"Fine. Now tell me."

"To the precinct on Main Street, of course."

"What's at the precinct?"

"Remember what the officer said? They were going to call the kidnaper in for questioning. I overheard them say about two o'clock."

"It's almost that time now," John announced quickly.

"Well, we better get rolling then," Willie commented and drove off.

About twenty minutes later, they reached the precinct on Main Street. Willie stepped out of the mail truck and walked inside the building. Mona and John waited inside the mail truck for Willie to return. The longer they had to wait, though, the more they grew even more impatient. Even minutes seemed like hours to them.

Although it wasn't long after Willie entered the building that John's keen eyesight spotted the kidnaper's brown station wagon. "Mom," announced John, "look over there. Isn't that the station wagon we followed yesterday?"

Mona lifted her head just enough to see what John was pointing at. "It sure is, John," she agreed with surprise. "He must be in there right now." Mona glanced over to the police station and saw a slender figure exiting the front door. "Quick, hide, it looks like he's coming out," Mona feverishly announced. They both ducked to the lowest part of the truck.

"Ouch," John yelled as he bumped his head on the cooler.

"*Sh*, John, he'll hear us."

"Mom," John tried to whisper, "are you sure that's him?"

"Yes, John. I'd remember that unshaven, pear-shaped, delinquent mug anywhere."

"When we were at the mall, you said you didn't think you would remember," John continued with a whisper.

"When you're upset, John, you'll say anything."

"Mom, where is he at now?"

Mona lifted her head enough to peep through the window. About that time, another figure, in a slumped position, exited the police station. He was holding his stomach like he was in severe pain.

"John, I know that can't be, but doesn't that look like Willie?"

John lifted his head a few inches to view the man coming out of the building. "It certainly looks like him, but why is he bent over like that? Do you think he's sick?"

"Maybe he doesn't want to be recognized."

"Sure, Mom, that does make more sense."

"Mona," whispered a voice from the opposite side of the mail truck. Mona leaped with questionable surprise as she turned to look.

"Willie? I thought," she said pointing toward the man in the crouched position. "Never mind," she said, shaking her head back and forth and then glanced over her left shoulder toward John with bewilderment on her face.

"What's the matter with you two?"

"Huh? Oh, nothing," Mona explained.

"I sneaked out the side door so he couldn't see me," he spoke with an anxious yet quiet whisper. "Did you see him?"

"Who?" asked Mona still in wonderment as she turned to the right to take another look at the man in the slumped position. This time the man, still in the crouched position, held his head up and looked straight at Mona. Mona and John were able to get a good look at his face this time and spotted a bottle of whiskey that he was clutching in his left hand. When they saw the face of this elderly Spanish wino, both Mona and John sighed with relief, "Oh."

"You got a problem, lady?" snarled the bum.

Mona shook her head no, and the Spanish wino growled and walked away. John giggled quietly.

"Mona," Willie became annoyed, "are you listening to me?"

"Yes, I'm listening to you, Willie. Did you see him?"

"Yes, Mona, I just told you that."

"Oh, sorry."

"Willie, quick get in. He's already in his car," John announced quickly as he observed the kidnapper's whereabouts.

"Then we've got to move fast. John, look back there and give me my white uniform shirt," Willie commanded as he opened the door and sat down in the compact seat on the driver's side. "I hope it's not wrinkled, but I guess I can't do anything about it now."

John reached for the shirt that was resting on top of the cooler and handed it to Willie. He helped his uncle put both arms through the sleeves, and then Mona helped with the buttons.

"Willie, did they tell you anything?"

"No, but I did get his name—Grover Clements—and I overheard two police officers talking about it. They said they would have to let him go for lack of evidence. And get this, they also said they couldn't hold him on suspicion alone."

"Suspicion!" yelled Mona. "Willie, we saw him take Joey. He was waving at us in the back of that man's brown station wagon. We even told them that!"

"I know, I know, but that's our story, Mona. They call that suspicion, not evidence."

"That's not suspicion, Willie. That's a fact. Three witnesses saw him with the evidence. Three!"

"I know that, Mona, but that's not the way the system works," Willie replied disgustingly.

"Well, screw the system," Mona announced, raising her arms in outrage. Willie's eyebrows jumped up so fast, they seemed to have almost lifted off the top of his forehead. He couldn't recall ever hearing his big sister speak with such vulgarity.

"I mean we're talking about a defenseless, innocent child here," Mona continued to disapprove and vent out her emotions. "My child!" she said pointing sharply at her chest. "And I refuse to give up, just because the police can't help!" Mona raised her voice.

"Whoa, Mama's mad now!" Willie proclaimed.

Mona shifted her head over toward Willie and whipped out a few brass words of bold, refreshing encouragement. "You bet I'm mad. We're going to kick those desperadoes right on their rear ends, knock them flat off their feet, and send them home crying for *their* mamas, right, gang!"

"Right on, Mad Mama! Yeah! GTC for sure," John joyously agreed.

"Right on! You go, Mad Mama!" Willie agreed with integrity but secretly lowered his spirits as he thought about what he just agreed to.

"I hope," he said quietly to himself so no one else could hear.

"Hey, look what I found," John interrupted as he spied something resting on the floor. It was pushed underneath the seat. John tossed his brother's green military ball cap over to his mother, and it landed right in her lap.

Mona grasped the cap that had "Joey" inscribed with black permanent marker inside the bill and squeezed it tightly in her hands. As Mona lifted the cap to her face, she could smell her son's scent that was worn into the fabric. Trying to hide her watery eyes, Mona bowed her head. Suddenly, a ton of weight pounced upon her heart. Trying to remain courageous and strong, Mona tried to hold back the tears that inwardly compelled to be released, but they were too forceful. "Willie." She sobbed, allowing deliverance to her emotional state. "Do you really think we'll find him?"

Willie looked into the rearview mirror and pierced his eyes at John. John looked back and motioned with his mouth and shrugged a gesture with his shoulders and palms up high. "What? I didn't know."

Trying to drive and keep a close eye on the kidnaper's car, Willie managed to search for Mona's arm, grabbed it with a tight brace, and softly but reassuringly answered, "Mona, I'm sure we'll get him back. Remember what you always told me when we were kids?" Mona shook her head with a short no answer and sniffled. "You always told me, 'Willie, there's nothing too big that God can't fix.' Remember?"

"I remember." Mona sobbed, blew her nose on a paper napkin, and lifted her head a little trying to hold back the rest of her emotions that were bottled up inside.

"I've never forgotten those words. Of all the crazy ideas you have come up with, this idea has always been the best yet. It has gotten me through many trials."

"That was the same day you caught the backyard on fire." She laughed. Willie grinned. "I'm sorry, I guess I just got scared."

"We're all scared, Mona, but we're not going to let those desperadoes make us give up. I promise you I won't stop trying until we get Joey back." Willie squeezed Mona's arm like a sponge and then placed his stray hand back on the steering wheel.

"Me, neither, Mom," added John.

Being reassured for the present moment, Mona leaned back to relax and collect her thoughts. Then she remembered the artillery. Knowing Willie wouldn't approve, she slinked her right arm in the crevice between the door and the front seat and reached her hand back as far as she could to the floor of the backseat. Finally, Mona felt something. She had found John's foot. John knew she was searching for the remainder of her apparel that Willie ordered her to take off before the trip, so he reached down and placed the explosive hardware in her hand. She smiled deviously and slyly redressed her outfit. Willie was unaware of anything Mona was doing. His mind stayed directly on the car in front of him.

"Okay, he's turning off the highway now. You two help me watch so I won't miss a turn."

Willie turned toward Mona and noticed she had redressed her outfit. "Mona," he snapped raising his voice, "you can't wear that in public!"

"Willie, calm down. No one will see me. I have to be prepared ahead of time. I can't wait until we stop."

"Oh, this is just great." Willie panicked with anxiety. "You have flipped. Now, I'm sure to go to jail this time. Only it won't be for speeding this time. Oh, no, I'll be harboring a crazed pistol packin' mad mama!" Willie said enraged and sped off faster.

"Willie, slow down!"

"Why? No one will see us. We're invisible today."

"If you want me to take it off, I will."

"You might as well leave it on now. We're probably almost there wherever that is."

"Willie," John yelled, "he's turning! You're gonna miss it!"

Completely turning with a screech, Willie pushed on the brake a little to slow down the vehicle.

"Where'd he go, John?" Willie panicked.

"Calm down, you didn't lose him. He's turning into those redbrick apartments up ahead. Just slow down, and park somewhere."

"Okay, you two get down in case he looks back this way."

"Willie, park behind that blue car over there," Mona ordered as she peeked out the window in an attempt to give directions with her pointer finger.

"Mona, that's too close. He'll definitely see me there. Will you get down!" he ordered.

"I'm just trying to help."

Well, you're not helping, so get down and be quiet."

"Then park somewhere already!" Mona impatiently barked.

"Will you two stop arguing? Willie, just park somewhere," John snapped.

"All right, I'm parking."

Willie pulled behind a white trans am about 150 feet away from the kidnapper's car. They remained inside the vehicle until the kidnaper walked far enough out of sight. As soon as he disappeared from view, Mona, Willie, and John jumped out of the car and ran to the left side of the building. Willie crept around the corner of the building to find an entrance in the same direction the kidnaper was walking. The stairway was positioned in the middle section separating two divisions of the apartment complex. Spying the kidnaper's whereabouts, Willie noticed every turn he made up the second flight of stairs.

"He walked upstairs," Willie gossiped in a whisper. "He's now turning left on the second floor. John, run up and keep a close watch on his next step."

"Okay, Uncle Willie," agreed John without question.

John ran up the stairs ahead of them while Willie and Mona waited for his signal to follow. As Mona and Willie waited and watched the stairwell intensely with their backs toward the street, someone from behind poked Willie on his left shoulder. Willie jumped and threw his arms up into the air as if he were under an arrest and shrieked, "Ah! Who are you? What do you want? We don't have any money, but we do have a lot of food. You can have it all."

"Willie, it's me, Mildred. Turn around." She laughed.

"Mildred?"

"Yes, your sister."

"Mildred?" Willie exclaimed, "What are you doing here?"

"And dressed like that?" Mona queried as she looked Mildred up and down and then stared into her painted clown face. Mildred was dressed in her new clown costume that Willie bought her for Christmas.

"Me? Have you looked into the mirror, lately, Mad Mama? I don't know about you, but I'm dressed for a birthday party two blocks down the street. I just happened to be driving by and saw you two snooping around the corner of the building. With what you're dressed in, Mona, I knew you two were up to something sneaky and adventuresome. That's why I stopped. I want to help."

"Oh, this is really turning out to be great," Willie jeered. "Is everybody costume crazy today? All we need now is a dancing ballerina in a pink tutu."

"Mildred," he advised, "go to your party."

"No, I want to stay and help. I'm early anyway. You two owe me. You guys never let me help when we were kids. I always had to watch. I don't want to watch anymore. I want to do something exciting. Who knows, you may need me for a diversion or something like that," Mildred said looking around as if she were the lookout person. "Please let me stay. I promise I won't get in your way."

"Oh, all right, you can come along, but you have to be quiet and stay out of sight." Willie construed.

"You'll never know I'm here. I promise."

"Promises. First John and now you," Willie mumbled.

"Huh?" Mildred said perplexed.

Just then a voice from the third floor stairway announced, "Mom, Willie, come on up, hurry." John looked down and then took a second glance with bewilderment frozen into his face.

"Where did the clown come from?" he asked himself.

When the group reached the third floor, John pointed to apartment number 35. "He went inside that apartment," he said as he kept staring at the new addition to their group.

"Okay, everybody," Mona informed, "let's do this like postal service." Mona glanced over at Willie. "You know, certified mail, so he'll have to open the door and sign for a letter or something."

"Oh, great, Mona! Let me guess whom you've chosen to play the postman's part. Oh, I know, you chose Mildred, right?"

"Oh, that's Mildred," John said surprisingly.

"Willie, can you come up with another plan?"

"No, I guess not."

"Then we continue with this one," Mona explained as she pulled out a letter from underneath her shirt. "Don't lose it, Willie. I haven't read it yet."

"I don't know, Mona, this is too risky," Willie complained. "What if he reads the name on the letter?"

"Uh…" Mona stammered as she thought for a second, "then, we'll just have to go directly to our emergency plan."

"Emergency plan? We have an emergency plan?"

"Well, yeah, but, Willie, we don't have a lot of time. Are we going to talk or deliver a letter?" Mona reminded him in an attempt to divert his attention.

"All right, but this had better work."

Willie approached the apartment door with caution. He tapped moderately two times with the brass-colored doorknocker. With the letter in his left hand and the doorknocker in his right, Willie attempted to knock a third time. Before he released the lever on the doorknocker, a voice yelled from inside, "What do you want? I'm busy."

"I have a letter for you, sir," Willie yelled back.

"Yeah, well, slip it under the door and go away!"

Willie thought a moment and replied, "I can't do that, sir. You have to sign for it. It's a certified letter."

"All right, all right, keep your shirt on," the man yelled back disgusted. A few minutes passed by; then, the doorknob began turning. The man behind the door opened it a few inches, stuck his nose out, and spied through the crack with one eye. He reached his arm out through the small crevice and signed Willie's tablet. Then he snatched the letter from Willie's fingertips and slammed the door shut.

Willie rushed back to the others and complained, "Well, Mad Mama, that worked great. I hope your emergency plan works better than this one."

"Emergency plan? Oh, yeah, well, I don't have an emergency plan completely worked out yet."

"What? You lied to me? Your own brother! Well, that's just great. I guess we go home, then. I don't know what else to do."

"Whoa, wait a minute. I didn't lie. I said I didn't have one completely worked out yet, but I believe I have another idea that just might work this time."

"Yeah, what is it? Are we using the mailman again? Maybe the bicycle contestant can go around collecting money for his trip? Or maybe the clown can sing a 'Happy Gram.'"

"Okay, Willie, calm down. I get your point."

About that time, John returned panting for air from an errand Mona had sent him on. He brought back a medium-sized parcel that was left in the mail truck from an undelivered attempt on Willie's latest mail route.

"Whoa, wait a minute, Mad Mama. That package is United States property. You can't use that." Willie grabbed the package out of John's hands and held on tight.

"Relax, Willie, you'll get it back," Mona demanded as she struggled with Willie trying to release the desperately needed package from his tight grip. "Willie, let go. It's the only way we can get him to open that door wider than an inch. As soon as we're inside, you'll get it back." Mona continued to argue her point, but Willie remained stubborn and held on with all his might. Nothing was going to pry his fingers from that package, and Mona knew it. Then without any warning, Mona lifted her fingers into the air and disgustingly wailed, "Fine, keep it." Willie sailed backward onto the concrete walkway with a despairing look upon his puzzled face.

"That's it. You give up. Oh, no, you don't give up that easily."

"Willie," Mona began to tear up, "wouldn't the US Postal Service be forgiving, if they knew it saved someone's life just to lose one package?"

"Maybe."

"Then for Joey, be an uncle right now and forget about being the postman. Remember whom you're doing this for. Please."

"And you promise we'll get it back."

"Would I lie to you?" Willie looked at Mona remembering her earlier lie to him. Mona stopped and stuttered out, "I...I mean I'm your sister, Willie. I wouldn't let you get fired."

"I wonder sometimes. All right, you convinced me. But of course, you always know how to get to me. Okay, let's do this like the postman, again."

"Thanks, Willie," Mona said and hugged her brother. "This time, Willie," Mona explained and touched the end of the parcel Willie was holding, "tell him you forgot this one."

"Okay, I'm going. Let's do it, before I change my mind."

"Okay, let's do it. Wait!" she excitedly agreed and then cautioned with a thought.

"What now?" each one said with disgust.

"Everybody, remember, don't use your real names. We don't want the kidnaper to know who we are."

"Anything else?" commented Willie sarcastically.

"No, that's it."

Willie turned again and approached the kidnaper's door boldly this time. He grasped the doorknocker with his palm and lightly tapped twice on the door. After a couple of minutes passed, Willie turned toward Mona, who was restless and motioning for Willie to knock harder. Grabbing the golden knocker in his right hand with much irritation in his action, Willie knocked twice again. Only this time he tapped loud enough to be heard.

"What do you want? I'm busy," the man yelled.

"Sir, it's me again, the postman. I'm afraid I've made a terrible mistake."

"I'll say you did," he snapped opening the door slightly with the chain stretched as far as it could reach. "That letter you gave me belongs to someone else. What kind of mailman are you? I aught to report you for this."

"Yes, sir, I know, but please don't. I have a package that actually does belong to you. This one even has your name on it," Willie commented with a little white lie. Little did he know, though, Mona had actually changed the label on the package to read the kidnaper's name and address.

The man yanked the chain from its latch, swung open the door, and snarled. He tried to snatch the package out of Willie's hand, but Willie wouldn't let go of it. "Well, are you going to give it to me or not?"

"You have to sign for it first, sir," Willie fidgeted.

The man took the tablet and signed for the package and then pried the package from Willie's hands. When he read the name on the package, Willie began to panic. "Uh, could I have the letter back, sir?"

"Hold on, don't be so pushy. I want to make sure my name is actually here this time." Willie began to get nervous. "And there it is. They always misspell my name."

"It is?" Willie asked puzzled. "Let me see. Oh, so it is."

"Hold on, and I'll get your letter." The kidnaper backed away from the door to get Mona's unread letter.

While he waited, Willie looked back to find the others but couldn't see them anywhere. *Where are they?* he thought to himself. *Mona better come up with the rest of the plan, or we're done for.* Then suddenly he jumped because a gun was thrust into his thigh. Looking down to see what was happening, he saw three marauders behind the door with artillery up in the air ready to barge in and take control. Willie didn't know whether to run away or faint. Willie shook his head at Mona and pushed the gun back toward her. "Mona, I don't want it," he whispered.

"Take the gun, Willie," Mona insisted, so Willie took the gun from Mona's hand and secretly pushed the gun into the back of his pants.

It seemed during the whole package drop-off scene, Mona came up with the rest of her emergency plan. She, John, and Mildred slithered side by side against the apartment walls, edging their way toward the front door of the kidnaper's dwelling. Mona gestured to Willie with her hands the next step to her emergency plan. So when the kidnaper returned to the front door with the letter, the four of them forcefully barged the door open, knocking the man back into one of the living room chairs. He landed with his legs dangling over the right arm and his head resting on the left arm. When he looked up to see what hit him, the startled man had to take a second look. His first glance was at the postman pointing a revolver and then John in his black leather jacket who was also pointing a pistol. He took one quick glance at Mad Mama tightly gripping a revolver in a "Don't move!" position and then stared questionably at Mildred, the clown, wearing a funny little hat with three bobbing flowers that continuously waved up and down at every move. Mildred was also pointing or actually shaking and waving a gun. The kidnaper, very much confused, shook his head back and forth. He looked back at Mona, lifted his hands in an arrest position, and asked, "I don't get it. What do you want from me, your missing tutu? I swear I didn't take it." He scoffed and looked back at Mildred's attire once more.

John, Willie, and Mona turned their heads and stared at Mildred. Mildred just smiled and shrugged her shoulders. "Here," she said to Mona, giving her the gun back, "you take this." Then she backed away two feet. "I'll just shut the door," she meagerly mumbled.

After Mildred closed the door, Mona moved a little closer to the kidnaper's face. She peered into the kidnaper's tired, brown eyes and snarled, "Okay, scum nuts, where is he?"

"Where is who, lady?"

"The little boy you stole from his mother at the mall yesterday."

"What little boy? I don't know what you're talking about. I haven't been to the mall since last week."

"Liar."

"Search for yourself, if you like, lady. There's no one here, except me."

Mona motioned for John to search the apartment, and the kidnaper decided to rise to a standing position. Mona gave him a hard kick in his stomach with her right foot and knocked him back into the chair again. He grabbed his stomach and grumbled in pain, "Lady, why did you kick me?"

"Shut up, scum nuts. When I want you to talk, I'll ask you a question."

About that time, John returned to the living room and shook his head at Mona indicating he found nothing.

"I'm losing my patience with you, scum. You better tell me what you did with that little boy."

"Look, lady, whoever you are," he answered, "I told you. I don't know what you're talking about. I don't even know who you are looking for."

"Oh, you know all right, you just won't admit it. When we get through with you, you'll talk."

"What's that suppose to mean?"

"Oh, just that we'll have to jog your memory a little. That's all."
"Oh, I'm really scared now."
"Wi-ell, Henry." Mona looked over at Willie almost forgetting to change his name for safety reasons. "You and Jake see if you can find some rope or something to tie him up."
"Okay," he agreed not knowing what else to say.
"All right, Mad Mama!" said John with excitement at first then changed his expression so no one could detect his enthusiasm.

Mona walked to the other side of the couch snooping around for clues. She thought maybe she could find a button or something. The kidnaper slowly began to rise trying not to be noticed, but Mona rushed over toward him, kicked him back into the chair with her right foot, pushed the gun into his forehead, and pulled back the hammer. Mildred watched frightfully.

"Who are you people?" he asked.
"You don't need to know. You made your first and last mistake when you took that child from the mall."
"Why? Who is he, the president's son?"
"No, but thanks for the confession."
"That was not a confession. I'll tell you just like I told the police, I wasn't anywhere near the mall that day. I went fishing with a friend, and he will vouch for me."
"Is that right? Well, you're one skinny, little lying runt," Mona yelled and slightly popped him on the forehead with the barrel of the gun.
"Ah," Mildred screeched.
"Ouch!" the kidnaper yelled and rubbed the wound with his left palm.
"Anyone can come up with a false witness," Mona yelled sternly.
"Good one," Mildred said admiring Mona's witty quick-to-the point comments.
"The mall is full of witnesses, stupid. That's where you made your first mistake. You were also seen leaving the mall with the child tucked away underneath a box. Oh, you certainly went fishing, all right, but it wasn't for fish, was it, scum?"

The kidnaper looked puzzlingly at Mona wondering how she knew about the box. He began to fidget a little as if he were trying to make his move and get away. About that time, John and Willie entered the room with some cords they jerked out of the blinds in the bedroom.

"This is all we could find, Mad Mama," John announced.

"Okay, then tie him up real tight."

The kidnaper began to feel uneasy and began inching his way to the edge of his chair again. Mona took out her PPK pistol and pulled back the hammer. Now she was holding two weapons; both pointed dead set at the kidnaper's heart. The man eased back into his seat again.

"Henry, get a kitchen chair," Mona commanded.

"Jake, you tie his hands and feet together and then tie him to the kitchen chair."

"Okay, Mama, whatever you say."

Willie brought the chair over and helped John bind the man's hands behind his back, and then they tied his feet together as Mona had requested. Willie and John lifted the man off the recliner and placed him onto the hardback kitchen chair. Another rope was attached around the man's waist securing him to the chair.

"Here, watch him," Mona said as she gave Mildred a gun and walked away. Mildred placed her fingers around the gun trying to hold a steady grip. While Mildred held the kidnaper at gunpoint, Mona searched the living room for clues. She reached down to pick up something when she heard a click from the gun. Mildred panicked and released the trigger, when the kidnaper made a sudden jerk. Lucky for Mildred, nothing happened, but the kidnaper, seeing that the gun was empty, began to squirm trying to set himself free.

"I guess you were lucky that time, scum," Mona said trying to think fast.

"I don't believe you have any bullets in that gun, and even if you did, your clown couldn't hit the side of a house," the kidnaper spoke snidely.

"Are you that sure of yourself? She may appear to be shaky and dimwitted, but what you don't see is a clown with an itchy trigger finger. That's why I always make sure the first round is empty. Go ahead and try to move," Mona calmly spoke at first. "This time the barrel's not empty." Then she whipped around toward the man and pointed a 9 mm to his head. This time, she spoke harshly, "I'd love to get off one round in your leg or your arm so you can bleed all over your ugly living room furniture, but it makes such a mess, and you'd have to clean up your own blood *'cause I don't clean scum.*"

Mona walked over to Mildred and whispered loud enough for the kidnapper to hear, "This time, Maxie, just watch him. Don't kill him yet. We still need him."

Mona walked over to the edge of the sofa again and reached down as if she were picking up something. Secretly, she reached behind her back to retrieve Joey's ball cap that she had stuck in the back of her pants prior to coming inside. Mona stood up holding the cap in her hands. "Hey, scum, look what I found," she said snidely as she lifted the object and shoved it in the kidnaper's face. "Sure you don't want to change your story?"

"That's Joey's ball cap!" Mildred gasped. Mildred didn't know about Mona's secret scheme, but John and Willie knew about the ball cap from the start. Mildred's innocence though expanded Mona's performance tremendously, because when Mona exposed the cap and Mildred gasped, the kidnaper panicked and began to squirm hoping to find a loose end somewhere in the ropes.

"Where did you get that?" he asked.

"Oh, I found it in your floor tucked underneath the back of your ugly blue sofa. Does this cap belong to you, scum?" she asked placing it in his right hand.

"Yeah, sure it does," he agreed.

"Really? Well, why don't we try it on your scrawny, little head? If you're lucky, it might just fit you," Mona announced her next step. She snatched the cap from his hand and made a harassing attempt to force the small band on his head. "You know, I don't think it fits you. It just doesn't seem to fit your enormously stupid head."

"Then it's probably my brother's. We both have caps that look alike."

"Really? What's your brother's name?" questioned Mona with a sneer.

"Uh, Joey," he said remembering the name Mildred called out earlier.

Mona placed the cap in the man's hands again. The kidnaper looked down at the cap and called out the name with amusement. "Joey! The name on the hat is Joey. Like I said, that's my little brother's name."

"Right," Mona softly whispered as she got into the kidnaper's face. "You see, scum nuts, I know you don't have a brother by that name. You probably don't even have a brother. Anybody as stupid and ugly as you wouldn't have a brother 'cause after you were born, your mama probably quit reproducing. The way I see it, scum nuts, you ain't got nobody. Your mama probably even lost your address," Mona continued to remark with confidence. She was beginning to really feel her part now. Mildred, John, and Willie just kept back out of her way and listened with puzzlement. They didn't know what to expect anymore than the kidnaper.

"Now, scum nuts," Mona said as she went to the kitchen, grabbed another yellow, four-legged aluminum kitchen chair, and sat down in front of the kidnaper, "let's make this a short visit, okay?" Mona pulled out a very large, twelve-inch hunting knife, softly slid her thumb over the sharp edge, and made a paper-cut slice into her thumb. The small cut began to bleed a little. Mona licked the cut. Willie's and John's eyes bugged out in shock, and Mildred's mouth widely dropped open in fright like she was going to scream. Seeing their freaked expressions caused the kidnaper to shriek with fear.

"You wouldn't want to make me mad, would you, scum? That wouldn't be very pleasant for either one of us. Well, at least not for you anyway." The kidnaper swallowed a big gulp in his throat. "Tell me again where that little boy is—the real owner of this green ball cap."

"I...I...I told you, I don't know." He hesitated at first but kept his story.

Mona got in a little closer to the kidnaper. She ripped open his shirt by sliding the knife through the button threads and then placed the cold, steel blade on his naked chest. "Maybe I can help jog your memory," she said with a soft whisper.

"What do you mean? What are you going to do to me?" the kidnaper asked Mona with a worrisome voice.

"Oh, now, scum, you don't need to worry. It won't hurt... much," Mona spoke with an aggressive killing casualness as she slid the knife from his chest and up toward his throat.

"Mo...Mama!" Willie yelled, almost forgetting to change her name as Mona requested. "What are you going to do?"

"Shut up, Henry," Mona commanded sharply, and Willie backed away as he was told. Fear struck his face as he stepped back out of Mona's way to allow her to continue with the interrogation. This action puzzled the kidnaper.

Mona moved the knife a little further up the man's neck, and he yelled, "Mama! If you kill me," he experimented, "you'll never find the boy."

"We're talking now. Good. Tell me where the boy is, and maybe I'll let you live."

"I can't!"

"Why not?" Mona asked angrily. "You're making me very mad, scum." Her eyes blazed with fury. Mona lifted the knife from his neck and pressed it close to his face. "Let's try this again, shall we? It's not healthy to make Mama mad. *Where's the boy!*" she growled with a shout and pressed the knife into his skin enough to pierce it and bring out a little flow of blood.

"I...I..." He panicked not knowing what to do.

"Tell her, mister, tell her," Mildred shrieked with fear.

The kidnaper gazed at Mildred's frightful face and took a quick glance at the fear that screamed from the other two faces. "I can't tell you, Mama. He'll kill me."

"Who'll kill you?" Mona asked as she pressed harder on the knife. The rage of anger flared up inside her as she continued to prod the man for answers. "If you don't tell me, I'll kill you," Mona continued with blood-chilling words of angered expression. "I'll split you open with this knife, and your blood will gush out like a geyser, and then I'll watch you die." The more intense harsh words of anxiety Mona revealed, the more intensifying the atmosphere. The kidnaper was horrified. Everyone else in the room was alarmed at Mona's unlikely character. Willie was glad he was on Mona's side. A large lump stuck in his throat, and no matter how hard he swallowed, it wouldn't go down. Mildred's heart began to beat a morbid song, and her knees became weak and shaky. She had second thoughts about coming along now. John, on the other hand, was amused at his mother's great terror-threatening capabilities. Even though his eyes were affright like the others, he was still enjoying every moment.

The kidnaper still refused to divulge any information, so Mona reached for one of her hand grenades. "Still won't talk? Okay, then I guess I'll have to blow you up instead," she continued with a growl as she placed a grenade in his mouth and pulled the pin. Everybody raced to the front door while the kidnaper struggled to get free. He mumbled words, but Mona couldn't understand him. She placed the pin back into the grenade and took it out of his mouth.

"All right! All right!" he squirmed dreadfully. "I'll tell you, but first put that knife down, okay, and put the grenade away?" Mona slid the knife into its pouch that she had buckled around her waist and hooked the grenade back on the loop.

"Okay, everything is gone. Now, tell me!"

"Mama," the kidnaper continued, "you're crazy!"

"You don't know the half of it," Willie cried.

Mona leaned toward the man's face and looked straight into his watery eyes. "You got something to say to me or not. Spit out the words I want to hear, or I'll grab my knife again and stick it straight down your ugly, scummy throat. You've wasted enough of my time."

"She will." Willie gasped excitedly. "Tell her what she wants to know."

Observing again the fright in Willie's responsive blue eyes caused the kidnaper to quickly respond, "Mr. Hodges, Mama! Mr. Hodges has the boy."

"Mr. Hodges?"

"Yeah, I sold him to Mr. Hodges for two grand."

"Two thousand dollars?" asked Uncle Willie. "That's all you got?"

Mona glanced over at Willie and gave him a "shut up" look. Then she continued with her questionnaire, "Where does this Mr. Hodges live?" she asked.

"Oh, Mama, please don't make me tell you that. Mr. Hodges is a powerful man. He'll kill me and not think twice about it."

"Look, scum, how can he kill you if you're already dead? The way I see it, you don't have any other choice. *Now tell me where he lives,*" Mona shouted louder. Grabbing the sides of his ripped open shirt with her left hand, Mona pulled out the knife again, but this time she lifted the knife toward his nose and poked some of the blade inside his left nostril.

"Mama," he called out in fright, "you don't understand."

"No, you don't understand, scum nuts!" she yelled throwing the knife onto the coffee table that was less than two feet away. The sharp edges of the knife stuck sideways into the wood fibers. Mona reached for the grenade again and shoved the end of the grenade in his mouth. As she held it there for a moment or so, she commented politely with a devious crocodile smile, "You won't feel a thing." Mona winked an eye and whispered closer to his left ear, "I promise."

"Wait!" he mumbled with fright trying to speak. Mona took the grenade out of his mouth to listen.

"Wait, I'll tell you," he quickly responded. "He lives at 367 Livingston Street," he replied a little reluctant.

"At 367 Livingston Street? I know where that is. Are you sure you're telling me the truth?"

"Yeah, that's it. I promise."

"Maxie, write that address down."

Mildred looked over at Willie and retorted smartly, "I suppose she's talking to me. Got a pen and some paper, Henry?" Willie reached in his shirt pocket and handed Mildred a pen and Mildred's unread letter for paper.

"You better be telling me the truth, scum nuts, because if you're not, I'll be back to finish this job, if you get my meaning."

"It's the truth. I swear!" he cried out with intense fear in his trembling voice.

"Okay, Jake," Mona looked at John and ordered, "you and Henry pick him up and put him in the hall closet. We can't let him go just yet. He might try to contact his boss."

"But, Mama, you're not going to leave me sitting here all tied up in this uncomfortable chair, are you? I told you what you wanted to know."

"No," she said reluctantly.

"Henry, lay the chair down on the closet floor," Mona ordered again.

"What?" gasped the kidnaper.

"Now you can relax until we get back."

John and Willie tied some more cords to his hands to ensure the strength of the bindings, and then they dragged him, chair and body, into the hall closet. The kidnaper wasn't happy with his arrangements as the whole trip into the dark closet he was yelling, "No, I don't want to go in the closet. Please leave me in here. I won't say a word. I promise. Please, Mama, please."

"Oh, one last thing before I go. Just so you'll know next time, Mr. Kidnaper, don't mess with mad mamas ever again 'cause the next one may be even madder than me." Mona tossed her son's hat at his face and swiftly walked away. The cap rolled down to the floor, so Willie picked it up and pushed the cap down trying to force it on the man's head. Then he and John laid the chair down in a reclining position with a short drop to the floor.

"Ouch! Who are you people?" the kidnaper asked. "Is Mad Mama your gang name or something?"

Without a single word, Willie slammed the door shut, locked it, and walked away. The kidnaper was still yelling from inside the closet. "Please, Mad Mama, don't leave me here. Let me join your gang. I'll get that kid back. Let me help you."

"You better put the rest of that cord in a kitchen drawer somewhere." Mona motioned with her right pointer finger looking straight at Willie. "Wipe everything down you touched. We don't want any evidence of being here."

Willie grabbed the cord, then took two steps back and looked at the speakerphone sitting on one of the end tables. Feeling like a vigilante, he reached down, picked up the telephone, and yanked the cord right out of the wall connection. Mona watched Willie's theatrical performance, but she didn't seem to be impressed. "Okay-e," she mumbled and walked toward the front door where John and Mildred were impatiently waiting to hurriedly exit the apartment building.

"Don't forget your package, Henry," she said and walked toward the door with the others.

Willie grabbed the undelivered package that began their whole masquerade and swiftly protruded out the front door with the others. Then the four costumed "vigilantes" hurried down the stairs and headed for the mail truck, except for Mildred. She'd had enough excitement for one day, and besides she had a birthday party to rush off to, so she parted company and headed off down the street without a murmur. The other three, whereas, had more unfinished business to attend. This was only the beginning of their escapade. John, Willie, and Mona climbed back into the mail truck and headed down the road in search for Livingston Street.

CHAPTER 5

MONA FINDS JOEY

The stakeout on Livingston Street took place a few feet from a beautiful redwood home that flared out with a deep Spanish flavor. Even the lawn ornaments hinted with the Spanish theme. Willie parked the mail truck across the street at a nearby community park. They were close enough to see the front lawn yet out of plain view from unwanted company. During their wait, a shimmering red Lamborghini with white pinstripes and a just polished black Trans Am pulled into the garage. John happened to be the first to notice since he and his schoolmates were into elaborate sports cars. John, along with his friends, draped pictures of sports cars to their lockers. "That's gonna be my next car," each one would say. "That's the one I'm gonna get when I get a job."

"Yeah, right," John would say to them knowing it wouldn't happen, but he walked away dreaming of it just the same. No one really expected to get one, so they held onto their dreams and decorated their lockers instead.

While John was reminiscing and stuffing his face full of stakeout junk food, Mona and Willie watched the house for movement. Nothing seemed to be happening on the outside of the house though. Two cars went in, but nothing came out. Mona knew she needed to get inside. *If Joey is there*, she thought, *they're not going to expose him to the public.* Mona continued pacing in her thoughts as she watched quietly, but not as patiently as Willie would have liked.

"Mona, would you please sit down. You're a dead giveaway in that outfit."

"Willie, I'm tired of waiting," she said annoyed. "This very minute, they could be planning to move my baby. If we don't do something fast, we're going to let him slip right through our fingers."

"Mona, what can we do? We don't have any other choice but to sit and wait until they make their move."

"But, Willie, what if they don't make a visual move? What if they go through the back door or take Joey through the garage. All we've seen are cars driving in and out. We'll never know if Joey is with them or not. We're just going to have to get inside someway, but how?"

"Well, we can't walk up to their front door and say, 'Hey, how you doing? Can we take a look inside your beautiful home? Oh, by the way, we're missing a child and thought he might have gone inside your house. Would you mind if we searched your house?'"

"Willie's right, Mom," agreed John.

Willie looked at John with puzzlement and gibbered, "Hmm, uh-huh?"

"But I see an easier way to get inside. Look!" John pointed to a paperboy making his rounds. They watched him collect money for the newspaper from every house on the right side of the block and then crossed the street to collect on the other side.

When the paperboy approached the house next door to the Hodges's home, John leaped from his seat and headed across the street.

"John, where are you going?" questioned Willie. "Come back here!"

"Just wait here," he muttered from a distance.

"Willie," Mona disagreed, "let him go. I see what he's up to."

"You do? Well, I wish someone would let me in on the secret."

Mona smiled at her brother and patted him on the back. "It's no secret, Willie, just watch. You'll catch on." Mona wasn't about to tell Willie anything, because she knew he would probably disagree and refuse to grant John the liberty of going through with his plan.

Willie sighed disgustingly and watched John as he approached the paperboy. Before the paperboy could step one foot on the Hodges's lawn, John stopped him and began questioning him about his duties. Since they were concealed behind an Asiatic willow tree that reaped long, weeping branches, no one from the Hodges house could see them conversing. Through his oral questionnaire, John learned that the paperboy was collecting payments from all his customers. That he already knew, but he also received other valuable information needed to continue with his plan. John paid the boy the amount Mr. Hodges owed for his paper and sent him on his way. After the paperboy walked up the hill and disappeared out of sight, John ran back to the truck. He grabbed a note tablet, jotted down some names and addresses, and then crossed them all out, except for the Hodges's address.

"Okay, Mom," explained John anxiously, "I'll collect the money for the paper, and if my plan works, I'll try to find a way to get inside. You be waiting outside behind a bush or something and wait for my signal. Then you can sneak inside and check around while I'm diverting their attention with something else.

"That's it?" Willie panicked. "That's your plan? How does she get back out?"

"I haven't figured that out yet."

Mona turned toward Willie and reassuringly commented, "Don't worry about it, Willie. Plans don't always completely come together at once. You're the getaway car, so be prepared for my signal. When I wave this, like mad you break your neck to get to us in this little truck," Mona told Willie as she waved her red bandanna up and down and began to walk away with John toward the Hodges's residence.

"Mona, I don't like this plan," Willie cried with unknown fear. "What if they catch you?"

Both Mona and John turned to Willie and at the same time answered back, "Call 911."

John made his way to the front door, knocked, and announced himself. A brunette-haired lady with a model's figure opened the door and led him inside as John hoped she would. Mona tried to remain quiet behind the gardenia bushes and patiently wait for John's signal, but the minute she sat down in a pleasant spot, insects began to crawl up her arm, and grasshoppers nested in her hair. Being still was not one of Mona's qualities. She was diagnosed as hyperactive when she was a child, and as she grew to adulthood adapted, but still remained in a hyper state at times. This was one of those times she couldn't adapt to her situation. She redirected the ants to crawl elsewhere and continued fighting with the grasshoppers for a while. Finally, the insects left her alone; however, Mona was not able to sit comfortably anymore. She turned her legs to one side and then to the other. Each time she moved, something would poke into her skin and cause irritation, leading Mona to rearrange her seating position again. As she tried to mold her body into a comfortable position, an unpleasant smell slowly drifted passed her nostrils.

"Oh, great, what else will I have to contend with?" she mumbled to herself as she noticed a pile of rottweiler's fresh manure resting upon the recently mowed grass a few feet in front of her. A breeze just happened to pick up the scent and drifted its repugnant odor in Mona's direction. Growing more and more miserable as time elapsed, Mona tried folding her legs Indian style like the kindergarten children do, but that didn't help either.

John, on the other hand, was quite comfortable. The lady that greeted him at the door led him to a large living room area and offered him a comfortable seat on one of the ten-piece couch sections of what appeared to be made of brown buffalo hide with horns protruding from both ends. Surrounding the remaining areas of the room, behind the buffalo couch, were built-in bookshelves and wall-to-wall books just waiting to be read and absorbed.

"You're not our usual paperboy. What's his name?"

"Oh, you mean Eric."

"That's right, Eric. Where is he?"

"Doing the other half of his street. I'm just helping him out. You can call him if you like. Oh, sorry, he won't be there right now. I guess I could come back later."

"Oh, no, that won't be necessary. How much did you say we owe?" she asked.

"Huh? Oh, seven dollars and fifty-five cents," answered John confidently as he read from the list that he had previously crossed out before entering the house. "Your husband pays by the month," he added, remembering what the paperboy told him.

The lady smiled and blushed with flattery, "Oh, I'm not Mrs. Hodges. I'm Linda, Mr. Hodges's secretary."

"Oh! I'm sorry, ma'am," John apologized.

"That's quite all right." She fluttered. "I didn't mind it at all. Wait here, and I'll be back with your money."

"Okay, ma'am, thank you."

"Why don't you call me Linda," the lady said with a pleasing smile and walked away. Her intriguing smell of roses seemed to have followed her out of the room, leaving only a small trace of perfume behind after her exit.

John watched as Linda exited the room and walked out in the hallway. A lady in a white uniform approached her with a question, and she assumed a concerned look upon her face. Linda looked back into the room where John was sitting and politely announced, "Just sit tight, dear, it may take a few minutes more than I had intended. There is an important matter I need to attend to first."

"Oh, no problem. Take your time. I'm in no hurry," John assured her knowing this could possibly be his only chance to get Mona inside. After Linda left from sight, he veered around the corner to make sure no one was around and then swiftly crept toward the front door. Voices were coming from the other side of the door, so he waited until the sounds were hushed before opening it.

Mona was still moving around and began making scratching noises as she moved. Two guards posted on each side of the house approached the front lawn with inquiry to the direction of the noises. With the same question on each man's mind, each guard met face-to-face from a distance and called out.

"Bill, are you making that noise?" called out the east end guard.

"No, did you hear something too?" the west end guard answered.

"Yeah, that's why I came around."

"Could have been the wind," he said. "I don't see anything suspicious."

"Yeah, nothing to worry about, I guess."

Both guards were still puzzled, so they hung around a few minutes longer to be sure. Mona was worried. She knew John would be opening the front door at any time. She tried to think of something to do, but no thought came to mind. At that very moment though, almost out of nowhere and just in time, an old stray cat screamed a shrill pitch and ran off knocking down an upright trash can. Both the guards, being satisfied with an answer, laughed and went back to their posts on the opposite sides of the building.

The talking shushed from outside the door, so John carefully opened it and peeked his head around. "Mom?" he whispered with a question. "Are you out there?"

Mona stood up from the gardenia bushes so John could see her. She placed her pointer finger over her mouth as a sign to tell her son not to speak. John did as his mother gestured and waved a "hurry up" motion with his hand. She quickly rushed to the door and slithered inside the house. Inside, Mona looked around to decide where to begin her search. The stairs seemed like a good starting point, so she pointed to the stairs for John to see where she was headed and then drifted out of sight behind the stairwell. Cautiously, Mona poked her head out and observed for the right moment to dash upstairs. Linda and the lady with the white uniform were approaching the top of the stairs to make a decline. They were in deep discussion. Mona darted back behind the stairwell and strained her ears trying to listen in on their conversation.

After they reached the bottom stair step, Linda stated, "Let me pay the paperboy, and I'll be right back." The conversation ended, and the ladies went in separate directions. After both ladies disappeared out of sight, Mona sneaked upstairs. Mona wasn't sure how much time she had available before the ladies returned upstairs; therefore, she tried to dash in and out of the rooms as quickly as possible.

As he secretly watched his mother disappear up the stairs, John sprinted back to the living room, where he was supposed to be all this time. A faint scent of roses approached his sensitive nose, an indication Linda was close by somewhere. Before John could sit back down in the same place on the buffalo hide couch, Linda appeared inside the hallway entrance, so he plunged down onto the nearest section he could find.

Linda entered the room smiling. She noticed John had changed seats, but she figured, being a young boy, he was just impatient and fidgety, especially since it did take a lot longer than she had expected. "Here it is, John, seven dollars and fifty-five cents," she said, handing him the money. "You know," she said, "for some unknown reason, you look awfully familiar. Have you collected money for Eric other times?"

John tried not to panic. "Oh, no, ma'am, I'd remember your beautiful face." John flirted.

"Thank you," she said pleasingly. "Oh, well, I may not remember right now, but I'll figure it out. I never forget a face, especially a cute one like yours," she added returning the flirtatious comment.

"Yes, ma'am, I mean Linda," John blushed. His face lit up bright red like the season.

"By the way, tell me again. Where is Eric? Is he sick?"

"No, ma'am, uh, Linda. Eric had to be someplace else today, so he made me an offer I couldn't refuse."

"What offer was that?"

"He promised me I could borrow his bike for the race tomorrow if I would help him collect his monthly dues for his paper route."

"I thought Eric was saving up for a bicycle."

"Huh, oh, he is…uh was, but he saved up most of the money, and his mother let him go ahead and get his bike. Now he has to pay her back instead." John thought quickly.

"I see," she said pleased with the answer, "well, I hope you win your race."

"Thanks!" John said excitedly. "With Eric's new bike, I can't lose. You should see it. It's really neat."

"I'm sure I will. Maybe you and Eric can drop by and show it off someday."

"Sure thing," he said with a smile, but the whole time he was really thinking, *Not a chance, lady.*

Linda smiled back at John and directed him toward the front door. On the way, John tried to think of someway to stay inside until his mother was finished searching for Joey. Then he remembered the paperboy's advice, "They'll give you milk and cookies, if you ask them."

John turned to Linda and politely queried, "Uh, Ms. Linda, I don't want to impose, but do you think it would be okay? I mean, Eric said sometimes you give him snacks like milk and cookies."

"Oh." She laughed. "Sure, come on into the kitchen, and the cook will get you something. You look like you could eat more than milk and cookies. What do you think?"

"Yes, that'd be great!" he tried to sound overly excited, but after eating all the stakeout junk food his mother stuffed in the truck, it was hard to be convincing.

Linda led John to a white swinging door. She pushed it, held it open a little for John to step through, and then let the door swing back shut after they entered. Linda gestured for John to sit on one of the kitchen chairs and whispered a few directions to a large breasted Caucasian woman with a medium frame and size 44 hips. Linda touched John's shoulder as she drifted out of the room. The cook looked over at John and smiled. "Hungry?" she asked walking toward him with a plateful of food items.

"Yes, ma'am!" he said with enthusiasm.

The cook placed a plate in front of John along with a tall glass of milk and then walked away to another part of the large kitchen and continued working with her back turned toward him. The plate held all kinds of goodies such as chips, fruit, cookies, and an enormous sub sandwich. John drank the milk down as fast as he could and stuffed the cookies and pretzels in one pocket of his jacket and the banana in the other pocket. Grabbing the sandwich in his left hand, John slinked down on the floor and crawled underneath the swinging doors. Still in a crawling position, he moved forward to the stairs like a dog. Voices from above the stairwell cautioned him to hide under the stairwell until the sounds disappeared into the hallway.

That same noise startled Mona in her investigation as she headed for the last room in search for her son. When she heard the two ladies talking in the upstairs hallway, she panicked. Not knowing where to hide, Mona just crouched behind a door and began praying for help. "Please don't let them see me, Lord, please don't let them see me," she prayed silently. The talking grew louder at first and then slowly drifted away.

"That should keep the little one quiet for a while." Mona heard one of the lady's comments. Her voice was somewhat muffled. "You should check on the others in about an hour," she continued. "They should be waking up about that time."

"Yes, ma'am," answered the second lady.

They continued talking as they walked down the stairs. "Light and lean," announced one of the ladies, "so that their little stomachs won't get upset so easily. You know, Mr. Hodges said the little boy threw up all over the car seat."

"No!"

"Yes, it was awful. They're still trying to get the smell out."

"Did they try disinfectant?"

"Yes, they tried everything. I guess it'll just have to wear out."

The ladies continued talking until they finally disappeared out of sight. Mona was in deep thought. She knew Joey had a weak stomach and hoped it was him they were talking about. "Yeah, throw up on 'em, baby," she said to herself proudly, but then tears began to flow as she thought of her little son.

Mona sobbed tenderly. "Oh, Lord, please let Joey be in that last room." Mona paused a moment and began to form larger tears that began to roll down her cheeks.

"What if he's not in there? I don't know where to go from here," she cried. "Oh, dear God, please let me find my son and take him home. You promise..." Mona paused a moment to catch her breath as she cried and whispered prayerfully, "You promise you won't put anymore on us than we can handle. Lord, I don't think I can handle anymore. Forgive me for being so rough on that kidnaper, Lord, and kicking him as hard as I did and so many times. But I figured he wasn't going to tell me anything, unless I disgruntled him severely. I'm sorry I lied to Willie and made him use his mail truck. Don't let him lose his job. Oh, also,

I'm sorry I made him eat mud pies when we were little and that grasshopper, in which I lied again telling him it was a small perch. And another thing I'm sorry about is the fire in the backyard. It was actually my fault, but I don't have to tell you that. Willie thinks it was his match that started the spark that burned down the barn and everything in it. I guess I need to tell him that, huh? Anyway, thank you, Lord. Amen."

After she ended her prayer of confession, Mona rose to a standing position and listened cautiously for noise; then, she peeked outside the door entrance, and no one was in sight or sound. Down on her hands and knees like a dog, Mona crawled on the floor of the hallway toward the last room. It was the only room left that she hadn't searched. Reaching for the doorknob, she turned it, but it was locked. She read in one of her survival handbooks how to open a locked door without a key, and she previously prepared herself for that purpose. Now, it was time to test her knowledge. Mona took out a small tool kit from inside her shirt pocket, pulled out an old plastic credit card, and then she pulled out a flathead screwdriver. Remembering the techniques in the survival handbook, Mona took the credit card, slid it in the crevice of the door, then pushed the straighthead screwdriver inside the keyhole and gave a few jiggles to the lock. It still didn't budge at first, so she tried a few more jiggles with the screwdriver. Then there was a snap, and the door unlocked. Mona joyfully crawled inside the room, closed the door behind her, and then secured the lock.

"It worked!" she said excitedly as she rose to a standing position. "Detective Mad Mama at your service," she mimicked in a whisper to her imaginary audience. "Here's my card." Mona held out the old plastic credit card she used to open the door and smiled. Before her eyes though were several beds. Four, of which, were seemingly occupied with small bodies. She approached the first three beds and uncovered their faces, but not even one resembled her son. One of the children was a girl about the age of ten, she guessed, and the other two were toddlers of the male gender, each about two years old. Mona admired their cute resting faces. She wished she could pick them up and cuddle them. "I know you miss your mommy," she whispered in the little one's ear and stroked his soft left cheek. Tears began to form in Mona's eyes as she gazed upon the child thinking of her own son.

Then the doorknob rattled and startled Mona. She quickly covered the children and crept fleetly to a nearby closet. The race to quickly get to the closet made Mona short of breath, so she gasped for air. Rapidly cupping her hand over her mouth, Mona tried to finish breathing and hoped the visitor didn't hear.

A nurse rushed inside the room frantically in search for something. "Ah, there it is," she said to herself as she grabbed her medical bag and then scampered back out again slamming the door.

Listening quietly, Mona heard her feet scuffling in the hallway and then down the stairs. Cautiously, Mona turned the handle of the closet door and peeked around suspiciously. With no one in sight, Mona gradually walked out. Returning for her final search with one child left, Mona approached the last bed with apprehension. She reached out to grab the end of the bed covers but pulled back her hands in fear it wasn't going to be Joey under the pale blue linen covers. Tears formed in her blue-green eyes. "Be brave, be brave!" she kept telling herself. Being nervy this time, she reached out again to pull the covers off, and the doorknob rattled as it turned. Since she was farther away from the closet, Mona couldn't hide there as she did earlier, so she ducked underneath the bed and draped the sheet over the side to conceal her body. The visitor at the door seemed to be very cautious entering the room as if he or she did not want to be heard. *Maybe they know I'm here,* she thought. *Maybe I made too much noise, and someone heard me,* she continued thinking of a solution. Mona was terrified but became very curious when she saw a pair of black tennis shoes stop in front of the bed where she was hiding.

"Black tennis shoes?" she questioned. "Would a nurse be wearing black tennis shoes with a white uniform? Although," she kept inquiring, "maybe they are just trying to throw me off… no, even I don't believe that." Mona tried lifting the blanket that was draped across the bed and hanging very low, so she could possibly get a glimpse of the person wearing the tennis shoes. As soon as she lifted the blanket, the unknown visitor noticed the mysterious lurker and bent over to get a good look.

"Aah!" Mona slightly screeched without vocal sounds. She mostly pushed air through her larynx, and her facial expressions made up for the loss of sound. "John? You scared the chowder out of me," Mona scolded.

"Me?" whined John, "you're the monster lurking underneath the bed. I thought you were one of the kids playing hide and seek or at least I was hoping."

Mona quietly laughed as she pulled her body out from underneath the bed and got to her feet. "I'm sorry I frightened you. When you turned that doorknob, I didn't have time to hide in the closet so that's why I hid under the bed."

"Oh," he laughed. "That's why? Why did you move the blanket though? I didn't even know you were there. You would have been caught for sure."

"I didn't think a nurse with a white uniform would wear black tennis shoes, so I took a chance hoping it was you."

"Did you find him?

"Joey?"

"Yeah, isn't that why we came here?"

"I searched every bed except for one. That's when you turned the doorknob, and I had to hide."

"Which one's left? I'll check it."

"No! Don't, John," Mona insisted. "It has to be me. I have to do this…for myself, okay?" John nodded in agreement.

Mona sat down on the left side of the twin bed; slowly she reached out to grab the blanket, and then she halted. "Maybe you better lock the door, John. We don't want any unexpected guests coming in." She stalled.

"Way ahead of you, Mom," he announced. "I locked it when I came in. What are you waiting for? Pull the covers off, or I'll do it myself."

"Okay, I'm going to. Just give me time."

"Time is what we don't have right now."

"All right, all right, I'll do it," she said and reached out once again to uncover the secret face. Her hands were shaking, and her eyes were closed. The closer she got to the motionless child's head, the more she shook. Getting almost there, she withdrew her hands.

"I can't," she said, "what if it's not Joey. I don't think I can deal with that."

"Mom, we've come this far. Now is not the time to give up. Think of it this way, what if it is Joey, and you miss the chance knowing?'

Mona cried softly. John grabbed her hand and said, "Let's do it together, okay?"

Mona smiled and shook her head in agreement. John guided his mother's right hand to the blanket as he reached with his right hand, and together, they pulled the edge of the covers down, exposing a motionless six-year-old male child, with a very familiar face. Mona's eyes were closed the whole time. "Mom, open your eyes. It's Joey," John commanded joyfully. Mona entreated his command and burst out into big tears of joy and gratitude.

"Joey, it's my baby," she cried softly. "Thank you, Jesus, thank you," Mona joyfully exclaimed aloud and then scooped her son up into her arms and held onto him dearly.

John smiled teary-eyed and enveloped his family into his arms. "I'm so glad we found him, Mom."

"Me too, John, me too," she said, and they both rejoiced holding each other with Joey's motionless body trapped in the middle of their embrace.

Then John broke away from the tight squeeze to give his mother some private time with her lost son. Mona held onto Joey dearly. She just couldn't let go. Every time she laid him down on the bed, Mona had to pick him back up and squeeze his motionless body again. While his Mom was catching up on hugs and kisses, John looked around the room for clues to help them escape. At the moment, there didn't seem to be a large selection, but John never gave up on anything in his life. He continued to investigate further until he came up with an infallible plan.

CHAPTER 6

ONE GREAT ESCAPE!

The search for Joey was finally over, but a plan of escape was yet to come. Even so, at this fastidious moment, Mona was not able to focus on evading the kidnaper's home. Her concentration was right in front of her, still and lifeless. Mona lovingly looked down upon her motionless son in amazement. She was pleased God sent her to the right house. Being so wrapped up in her glory, Mona reached across the bed, grabbed her little son's body again, and tightly embraced him. His nonemotional state didn't seem to bother her as she continued to cuddle him longer.

While John looked around the room in search for ways to escape, he watched Mona grasp Joey with tender motherly love, the type of love that is unbreakable. He didn't want to arouse his mother's soul-stirring moment with his brother, but time was running out for the three of them. He knew if they didn't retreat quickly, they would all face danger or death.

"Mom," he whispered anxiously but with compassion, "I don't want to spoil this moment for you, but we need to come up with an escape plan and get the heck out of here. Like now!"

Mona looked up at John with tears streaming down her cheeks. She grabbed John with her left hand still holding onto Joey with her right and gave him a tight motherly squeeze and then released. "Well, then," she said gladly, "let's find one and get the heck out of here." Mona laid her son back down on the bed and began helping John search for an escape route. As she and John looked around the room for ways to escape, they envisioned the other three sleeping children.

"Mom, are you thinking what I'm thinking?"

"Probably, but I don't know how we're going to do it."

In their hearts, Mona and John knew not one child could be left behind, so they pondered a moment in deep thought hoping to come up with a solid, fail-proof plan.

"John!" Mona suddenly remembered. "I saw an escape ladder in the closet where I hid the first time. We could use it to climb out through the window."

"Sounds good to me," agreed John, and he walked over to the closet to get the ladder. He took it out of its box and tried to quietly unravel it. After securing one end to the ledge of the opened window, John draped the other end gently over the side of the house. The end rung reached only three quarters of the way down. "Mom, it's not long enough," he said, looking around the room. "We need about six feet of rope or something. Ah! Grab some of those sheets from the beds, Mom." He pulled up the escape ladder and tied a few bedsheets to the end rungs on each side. Then he tied some knots in the sheets about one twelve-inch rule apart.

After returning the reconditioned ladder to it's outside position, John observed the length was still too short. "It's still not going to be long enough, Mom," he said.

Mona looked out the window to observe the leftover space to the ground. "That's not very far. We'll just have to drop the rest of the way. We need the rest of the sheets to tie the kids around our waists."

"Okay."

Mona easily released two more sheets from underneath two of the slumbering children. She tied the ends of one sheet around her waist. "Okay, John, put the two babies inside the pouch and tie the ends off like this," she said, demonstrating for John to crisscross the ends around her chest, underneath her arms, and then tie off the ends in the back. John understood her exhibition and gathered the two babies one at a time placing them into the cocoon-like compartment. Then he crisscrossed the sheet and tied the ends in the back with a double knot as Mona requested. "Now," she continued, "take that other sheet over there and tie your brother to your back."

"Mom, what are we going to do with her?"

Mona looked around and spied one child remaining. "Oh! Well, we can't leave her. Do you think you can carry her in front? She's much too heavy for me."

"Yeah, I think I can carry her too, if there are enough sheets," he said trying to locate another sheet.

"Check the closet," Mona suggested.

John pulled out an extra set of sheets from the closet and began tying it around his waist. As John tied the last knot of his heavy load around his waist, a rustling noise was heard outside the door. "Mom, did you hear that?" he whispered.

"Yes, I did," she whispered back. Both stopped working and listened for a few seconds, but not another sound was heard.

"I guess it was nothing," Mona suggested.

"Maybe, but let's barricade the door with something just in case. That'll give us more time to get out the window."

"All right, John, but let's jam the lock first. Reach in my left pocket, your right, and take out my utility box." John followed his mother's instructions.

"Okay, now on the opposite side pocket reach in and give me the tube of quick drying cement glue."

"GTC, Mom, you really dressed the part, didn't you?"

Mona smiled at her son and commented, "You know I always like to be prepared."

"Yeah, well, Willie thinks you read too much."

She smiled and commented as she opened the tube of cement. "The books are what give me inspiration, knowledge, and know-how." Mona squeezed the entire tube of cement into the small keyhole, put in an old key that she had taken from the utility box, and twisted it until it broke off inside the lock. "Otherwise, I wouldn't know how to do what I just did."

John agreed and walked away in search of something to block the door. He spotted an old heavy dresser. "Perfect," he said to himself as he grabbed a blanket, laid it down on the floor, and fed the ends underneath the legs of the dresser.

"Okay, Mom, help me slide this dresser in front of the door." Mona and John smoothly slid the dresser in front of the door entrance, pulled out the blanket, and headed for the window. As she waved the red bandana for Uncle Willie to see, Mona carefully stepped out onto the rungs, squeezed a tight firm grip with both hands and began climbing down. John waited for his mother to get half of the way down before he made his exit out of the window.

Heeding the red bandana Mona waved, Willie turned on the ignition and, as Mona requested, drove like mad toward the house. An armed guard was posted on the left side of the house, the side where Mona was skimming down what appeared to be a rope. Willie panicked, "Oh, no, they'll shoot her!" In order to focus the guard's attention away from Mona, Willie drove onto the front lawn like he was drunk knocking over a few lawn ornaments and crushing a few flower bushes. Then he quickly detoured to the right side of the house hoping the guard would follow. The guard ran after him shouting out commands to the guard that was posted on the right side of the house, "Jim, stop him!" Jim, the guard posted on the west side of the house, began chasing after Willie also. Willie circled around to the back of the house and within centimeters missed taking a drive into the swimming pool. A few lawn chairs took a free ride on the small mail truck, and a few obstacles splashed into the pool, but Willie finally reached the east side of the house where he spied John humpbacked trailing down the ladder and Mona was dangling off the side of the house from a rope about ten feet up.

During this time, Mr. Hodges's secretary, Linda, sat quietly on the buffalo hide couch trying to recall where she had seen John's face. Mr. Hodges, a handsome man with broad shoulders, small waist, and large hands walked through the hallway and noticed his secretary in seclusion. With much curiosity, he announced, "You're awfully quiet today, Linda. Are you ill?"

"Huh, oh, no, I was thinking about that paperboy today."

"Isn't he a little young for you?"

Linda smiled. "Oh, I remember now," she said assuredly to her boss.

"Remember what?" he questioned.

"That face. I knew he looked awfully familiar."

"Yeah, go on."

"You know that little boy that threw up in the car?"

"Yeah."

"The paperboy that came to collect for Eric today looks just like him. Like they were close kin. So close they'd pass for brothers."

"Really? And where is this paperboy now?"

"I don't know. Although, he could still be in the kitchen."

"What? Get upstairs and check on those kids. Something doesn't seem right."

"Yes, sir," she commented and ran towards the stairs.

"Brad," Mr. Hodges called to one of the men posted inside the house, "see if the paperboy is still in the kitchen and bring him to me."

"Yes, sir."

Linda and the nurse in the white uniform ran up the stairs together. When they reached the bedroom door, each shared some difficulty in opening it. "It's locked," Linda said thinking everything was okay since the door seemed secure.

"It's locked, Mr. Hodges," she yelled down the stairs.

"Then use the key and unlock it!"

"Duh! As if I wasn't going to," she said sarcastically and inserted the key with a hard left turn.

"It's stuck," she yelled. "I think it's jammed from the other side, and there's something…gooey inside the keyhole," Linda commented as she paused and lifted her hand exposing a clear solution running down her palm. She grabbed the doorknob to turn it, but couldn't release her hand from it. "Ah…I can't get loose. I'm stuck."

Mr. Hodges and three other men trampled up the stairsteps, and Mr. Hodges shouted, "Linda, get out of the way."

"She can't," yelled the nurse, "she's stuck to the handle."

"We need some fingernail polish remover," explained the nurse.

"That'll work." One of Mr. Hodges' men smiled. He changed his smile to a frown and lowered his head when Mr. Hodges turned toward him with a puzzling expression.

"Check my purse in the hallway," Linda exclaimed.

The nurse fled down the stairs, grabbed the purse, and, in a panic, emptied out everything. She grabbed the polish remover and dashed back up the stairs. "Here," she said out of breath and handed the polish remover to one of the men. He unscrewed the lid and poured the solution on the doorknob. The polish remover caused Linda's grip to loosen and allowed her to pull away.

"Thanks," she said, trying to rub off the rest as she backed away. "This feels awful."

"Try biting it off," said the nurse, trying to remedy the situation.

Mr. Hodges's men took turns trying to bust in the door with all their weight, but neither man was fortunate.

John almost jumped out of his skin when he heard the first bump against the door. He began stepping down faster and yelling, "Mom, hurry, they're coming!"

Mona released the ropelike sheet and dropped to the ground landing on her backside. She got up holding her back and looked up at John. "Hurry, John, hurry!" she yelled.

The door gradually broke open; each man forced his body inside and began searching under the beds and in all the closets.

"Not in here, stupid, out there," Mr. Hodges said pointing out the window. When they looked out the window, John was almost all the way down. One of the men grabbed his gun and started to shoot at John, but Mr. Hodges stopped him.

"Wait, you might shoot one of the children. Go around the front before they take off in that little bitty truck."

"Yes, sir, they're as good as gone," replied Bart in his deep voice. He was stoutly built and muscles protruded out of his short sleeves. His face looked as though he hadn't shaved in a week, and his hair was tied in a ponytail. Bart walked out of the bedroom and headed toward the front door. When he opened the door and stepped outside, someone hit him on the head from behind with a helium tank and knocked him out cold.

"There," she said proud of her maneuver, "that'll help them get away." Mildred, still dressed in her clown suit, ran back to her apple green Ford mustang and waited for the getaway to commence. After the birthday party was over, Mildred decided to take a tour down Livingston Street so she could help out in case she was needed like she did the last time. This time, she was right. That bop on the head slowed down the kidnaper and gave Mona and John more time to escape down the ladder and into the small truck.

While Mr. Hodges waited for his man Brad to surprise Mona from the front, John was almost all the way down. He had reached the homemade sheet ropes, and the rest of the way down was an abrupt slide and then a hard thump to his right side.

"Ouch, that hurt," cried the girl in the front pouch. She slid out one of the side openings and was tossed to the ground.

John looked surprised. "I'm sorry," he said. "Are you okay?"

She stood up and shook her head yes. "Where are we going?" she asked.

"We have to get away from the bad guys."

"Oh, okay," she said, being satisfied with his answer without a care.

Mona lifted the bundle off her head and passed the babies over to Willie. Willie grabbed each one and gently tossed them in the back of the truck. After lifting himself off the ground, John untied the sheets, lowered Joey off his back, and passed him over to Willie.

Willie kept yelling, "Get in! Get in! They're coming after us, and they have real guns, Mona, real guns!"

John turned toward the ten-year-old girl and quickly retorted, "Hurry, get into the truck." The little girl did as he requested without hesitation.

Just as Mona and John started to step inside the mail truck, the two guards came running around the corner still chasing after Willie's mail truck.

"Hold it right there, lady. Don't move, you or your boy."

Mona carefully lifted her hands above her head. Exposed in her left hand was a hand grenade. Her right pointer finger was looped inside the pin. "Uh, gentlemen," she said as she turned slowly to face them, "you really didn't think we came here unarmed, did you? I wouldn't think of shooting if I were you. Now throw down your little guns, and back up far enough away so that you can't reach them—about fifty feet will do."

"She's bluffing. If she pulls that pin, she'll kill us and her family," announced one of the men. "Do you really think she's going to do that?"

Mona overheard and commented, "I'm not bluffing. I'm just a little mad. You see I'm not going to let you take my son away from me again. If I can't have him, you can't have him either. I'd rather he be dead with me than be sold or molested with you. So what's it gonna be, fellows? Make it quick, guys. I really don't have much time."

Both guards looked at each other with hesitation. Mona smiled and commented,

"Okay, I warned you both. Surely one of you has some common sense. One yank on this ring, and you're history. It could get really messy. One of your legs would be over there." Mona tilted her head in separate directions as she spoke, "Your guts might be splattered on the side of the house, and your arms would probably be miles apart."

One of the guards expressed a bit of fear and anxiety, while the other guard still questioned Mona's sincerity. They mumbled back and forth to each other. Finally Mona yelled, "Forget it, guys, I'm getting impatient. Either we leave or I pull. Either way, I don't care. It's your call." Mona waited and then called again, "Okay, ready, at the count of 3, 1, 2…"

"Wait!" the fidgety guard yelled. "We give up." He laid down his gun and backed up about fifteen paces and stopped. The other guard hesitated to do the same but followed the same action and backed up also.

"Mr. Hodges isn't gonna like this," he said.

"Yeah, well, Mr. Hodges doesn't care if you or I die, so I don't care what Mr. Hodges likes. I took this job to protect Mr. Hodges. His life isn't in danger right now, is it?"

"Okay, guys, one more thing. You have to take down your pants. Go on, you heard me." Each guard began unbuckling their belts. "That's good," Mona agreed.

"Get in, John, hurry up," Mona quickly whispered. John did as his mother said but watched cautiously to grab her in case she needed help.

"Good job, boys! Did anyone ever tell you that you have cute knees? Well, they were wrong. 'Bye now." Mona heard a noise above her head as she stepped one foot inside the little truck, and John pulled her inside.

"Look, they're getting away," yelled Linda from the bedroom window.

"What are you two doing with your pants down? She's just the mama, get her," Mr. Hodges yelled down to the guards.

"Wrong, I'm the Mad Mama," Mona called out an earsplitting yell as she hung out the small side window.

"She's taking this too far," John said as he reached out, grabbed his mother's collar, and yanked the other half of her body back inside the mail truck.

"Hit it, Willie!" he yelled.

"On my way," he replied. Willie spun out, dug up some grass roots, busted some concrete flowerpots, and knocked over a ceramic matador and his bull. Then as he drove onto the street, he met an oncoming red jeep and ran him off the road. All the while, Willie was flinging the lawn chairs that were attached to his truck when he was poolside.

"Crazy driver!" yelled out one of the passengers in the red jeep.

The two guards in peril tried to pull up their pants but tripped over them in a frenzied approach to retrieve their guns and shoot. When Mr. Hodges noticed they were all tangled up, he ordered his other men to catch up with the mail truck and get the children back.

"Those kids are worth millions! Get them back!" he strongly commanded. "I don't care what you do with the others," he said angrily. "Just get those kids back. Where is Brad? I sent him out there ten minutes ago."

In an attempt to catch up with Willie, the second group of men jumped into a black Trans Am and took off passing the red jeep, running him off the road. He attempted to get back on the road again but was forced off the road for the third time by Mildred's late model apple green mustang. This time he was so mad he chased after the mustang that was following the black Trans Am in the mad dash for the mail truck.

The black Trans Am behind Willie was advancing rapidly. The passenger inside the vehicle held his right arm out of the window and began shooting at Willie's truck.

"Watch out, Willie!" John yelled. "He's aiming for the tires."

"I know, I see him, but I'm driving as fast as I can."

"Then drive faster," Mona yelled.

"Mom, this little mail truck won't go any faster," John explained.

"Then we need to get another one somehow."

"Yeah, right," John sarcastically agreed. "No problem. We'll just use Aunt Mildred's high-powered mustang. She's probably right behind us. Good thinking, Mom."

"Yeah, the time we need her the most, she decides not to follow us," ironically remarked Willie.

Willie tried pushing down harder on the gas pedal, hoping to gain some speed. Then all of a sudden, the little mail truck took off in a faster rage of speed that Willie almost lost control. Not having the experience of driving the truck any faster than it's normal speed caused some difficulty holding it on the road. The truck shifted from side to side giving them the ability to dodge the rapidly flying bullets with eminent success.

"All right, Willie!" John joyfully expressed his concurrence with Willie's rocky maneuver, not knowing Willie was just holding on as the truck created all the shifty actions.

The passengers, also, were being jerked from side to side. "Willie…careful. You're…wreck the truck," Mona yelled as she swayed from side to side, and her words came up higgledy-piggledy.

Startled at first, Willie began to feel differently, and his face suddenly lit up a devious smile. "Cool your larynx, Mama," he cried dementedly. "Wild Willie is now in control. We're moving out, ye-ow!" Willie bellowed making a fist with his right hand and shooting the pointer finger straight up into the air.

John glanced over at his mother with puzzlement on his face. He shook his head back and forth and said, "Dementia." Mona flinched and began biting off her fingernails.

After two blocks had passed, Willie checked his rearview mirror for unwanted company. "Mona." Willie panicked again. "They're still behind us, plus a dark-blue Camaro has joined our group. What are we going to do now?"

"Willie, I thought you had everything under control. Sounds to me like you lost it back there somewhere."

"Mona, this is not the time to be sarcastic. If you have any suggestions, now is the time to speak up!" Willie began to worry.

"Calm down, Uncle Willie. We'll think of something. You just keep driving," John commanded.

"Do you think I have any other options?"

"Wait a minute! Willie, there's a sharp curve coming up ahead, isn't there?" Mona declared with an energized voice that began with a shout.

"Yeah, what about it?"

"Well, isn't there an alley that turns off to the right on that same curve?"

"Yeah, she's right!" agreed John excitedly.

"But it's too small for cars to go down it."

"Yeah, but not for little mail trucks."

"That's right! Perfect, Mona! Good thinking," said Willie with lots of enthusiasm.

"Okay, everybody hold on tight," Willie warned his passengers.

"Aah," screamed Mona as Willie squealed the tires on the pavement by making a quick left curve and then a sharp right turn into the alley. Each passenger shifted back and forth like a can of salmon being shaken vigorously from one side to the other.

The tailing vehicles didn't notice Willie's quick maneuver to the right into the diminutive alley. They continued to progress forward down the same street. Willie drove to the end of the alley and stopped. "We'll have to figure out what to do next, 'cause they'll be headed down that street in front of us in about seven to ten minutes depending on the traffic." About that time, a late model mustang cut them off at the exit. It was Mildred. They were so happy to see her smiling clown face and her funny hat that was still bobbing up and down.

"Mildred? You must be clairvoyant." surprisingly questioned Willie.

"Mildred, what are you doing here?" asked Mona.

"Hey, is that the greeting you give to someone who's about to save your life?"

"What do you mean?" asked Mona.

"If you guys exchange vehicles with me, I'll lure the bad guys away from you so you can make a safe getaway. After all, they're looking for you, not me. They don't even know who I am."

"That does seem to be the only option available at the moment. What do you think, Willie?"

"Let's go for it, but we'll have to move fast. It won't be long until they'll be coming around that corner, and I don't want to be here when they do."

"John?"

"GTC! Let's do it!"

"Okay, then everybody out and start shoveling little bodies."

After the babies and both children were shuffled from one vehicle to the other, Mildred hopped into the mail truck, and the adults entered the mustang. Each vehicle went into different directions. The mail truck turned left toward the tailing vehicles to lure them away in the opposite direction, while the mustang went straight and then turned right down the next intersection.

The red jeep that was tailing Mildred gave up when the shooting began, but the black Trans Am and dark-blue Camaro continued the search. The men in the Trans Am spotted the mail truck and made a U-turn in the middle of the street. The Camaro followed their lead. Mildred drove on a little faster to tease them. She continued driving a few blocks and then turned into the nearest police station, parked the truck, and hopped out quickly. One of the men got out and started following her. Mildred turned around, with her flowers bobbing expeditiously in front of her face, and confronted the man. "Hey, are you following me? 'Cause if you are, I'll scream, and they'll come out and shoot you," she said pointing her finger and staring into his eyes.

"Look, lady," he said, "we were following that, uh, a mail truck just like yours, and it disappeared. We thought you were it. You didn't happen to see one, did you?"

"No, I didn't. Why are you chasing mail trucks anyway? You're not one of those weird postal people, are you?" Mildred looked down at her watch and lickety-split spat out the words, "Sorry, can't talk now. I'm in a hurry and already late."

"What would you be late for at a police station dressed in a clown suit?"

"A party, of course," she yelled back toward the man. "Sergeant Mender just got promoted to lieutenant."

"Oh," he said, satisfied with her answer and walked away.

After Mildred swiftly walked out of sight, the man walked over to the mail truck and peeked inside. He saw the cooler and a few bags filled with food items. They didn't seem to interest him though, so he walked away and went back to his car.

"Anything?" asked the driver.

"Nah, nothing, but..."

"But what?"

"I don't know. Maybe it's nothing, but why would a clown have picnic items in a mail truck and why would a clown be driving a mail truck at this hour anyway?"

"I don't know. It could be one of those singing telegrams."

"Maybe, but she seemed to have come out of nowhere, just when we were chasing that other mail truck and pretty much on the same street. Something just doesn't add up."

"Maybe we better check her out and see what she's up to."

"Right. Let's wait until she comes back out."

In the meantime, Willie was parked nearby watching to make sure Mildred was safe. "Mona, they're not leaving," he said worriedly.

"Okay, Willie, drive by so they will see us and leave Mildred alone."

Willie drove at a discreetly dawdling speed down the street that passed in front of the police station. He and Mona turned their heads in the direction of the two men that were chasing them. Mona showed a startled expression on her face so they would recognize her and begin chasing after them. As the plan took effect, Willie sped up faster, and the black Trans Am and dark-blue Camaro commenced tailing behind them once again. Within minutes, a red Lamborghini that was parked in the Hodges's parking garage caught up with them and followed the train of cars also.

"Mona, now that Mildred's safe, we're in deep trouble. Look! Now there are three cars tailing behind us, and I think they're all from Hodges's house."

"Okay, Willie, just keep calm and keep driving as fast as you can. We'll try to come up with a plan to lure them in the wrong direction."

"I hope you do it quickly 'cause we're fixing to run out of road."

While Willie drove at top speed, Mona and John thought wildly for a scheme to allure the file of cars that were tailing behind them. At the moment, the trailing cars were far enough behind to give them the edge for a safe getaway. They just needed enough time to figure out a plan of escape. Warily, Mona glanced back on occasion knowing time was not an option. She tried to settle down, but somehow the thought of desperadoes in the rearview mirror didn't help her self-control. Although, biting her nails seemed to calm her down a bit. John, however, remained in a relaxed state as he pondered their situation. He always contained his cool during dramatic climaxes. Of course, Uncle Willie continued getting the willies.

CHAPTER 7

THE RACE OF TIME!

Tension began to build as John and Mona remained quiet in deep thought while Willie drove like the howling wind down the highway, hoping one of them would come up with an idea quickly. He couldn't hold his peace any longer. Willie became drastically impatient, which annoyed Mona significantly.

"You see that sign up ahead? It means we're out of options, and if you two don't come up with one, we're dead," Willie alarmingly yelled.

"Okay, Willie!" Mona yelled intolerantly.

"John, got any ideas?" she yelled.

"Actually I do."

"You do!"

"Tell us," both Willie and Mona spoke in unison.

"The stadium."

"That's a perfect place to hide," agreed Mona. "Willie, let's play ball."

"Am I hearing you correctly? You actually want to go to a football game?" Willie sarcastically commented.

"Yeah, Mom," snidely added John. "You can't turn the picture off or turn the sound down when you get tired of hearing it. Remember, this is a real live football game."

"Okay, you two give it a rest."

"Wait a minute," said Willie puzzled, "I don't remember the way from this direction."

"I do, Willie. I'll direct you." John reassured.

"If you have to give directions, that may slow us down," Mona commented.

"Then, Mona, what do you suggest we do?"

"I'll drive," answered John.

"You'll drive?" asked Willie.

"Yes, I'll drive. That's the only way I know how to get there faster."

"John," smarted Willie, "if you haven't noticed, we are being chased by men with guns. Real guns! We don't have time to pull over and switch places."

"We don't need to, Willie. We can switch in transit."

"You mean while the car is still moving?"

"Of course, that is unless you want to pull over and ask those nice men with real guns to wait until we switch places. I'm sure they won't mind."

"Okay, you got me. What do I do?"

"I'll slide under you as you move to the right. We have to do this quickly, so when I call switch, you move fast. If you hesitate to move, we could have a wreck. Are you ready?"

"No, but I guess I don't have any other options. All right, let's do it."

"One, two, three, switch!" John called and slid underneath Willie's lap.

"Ah, wait, you've got my, oh, John!" Willie called discomfortingly. Somehow, Willie lifted his left leg up too high and caught his pants leg on the gearshift. He wiggled and moaned but managed to get loose. Then he attempted to swing his left leg over to get out of the way and blocked the driver's view.

"Move, Willie, now!" yelled John.

"I can't! I'm stuck, and I can't…" Willie garbled with a quick swallow of his own words.

"Would somebody do something quick. They're right on our tail," Mona shouted while watching the rear.

John reached over and grabbed Willie's foot. He gave it a sharp jerk throwing Willie across to the other side of the car.

"Watch it, will ya," he snapped.

"Sorry," John apologized reluctantly. "Maybe it would be a good idea if you put your seat belt on."

"That's not just a good idea," Willie answered as he buckled up, and the chase began full speed once again.

John turned sharp curves, made brisk turns, and outdrove like he was competing in the Indy 500 in an effort to escape from the tailing caravan. Still, he couldn't shake their advancing. A quick jolt and smooth turn into a car wash building kept them safe for a short while until the car waiting in line behind them placed money in the meter, which started the wash. Mildred's mustang began moving on the conveyor track toward the wash. Soap and water sprayed harshly inside the opened windows. Everyone rushed to crank the windows, but the water had already drenched them head to toe. The chill in the air made the splash uncomfortable. The babies began to cry because they were now cold and wet. Mona found a blanket and covered them up the best she could.

"I guess we better find another hiding place. Any ideas?" asked John.

"Not at the moment, but let me think a minute," answered Mona. "Willie?"

"No, I…I…" was all he could say as he shivered in the cold, wet climate that broke upon him.

"John, what about the Pastel Parade? Isn't that today?"

"Yeah, Mom, I believe it is. Hang on. I'll try to maneuver us into the parade without being seen."

John popped out of the car wash and turned onto the road again. The traveling caravan spied their vehicle and charged after them in hot pursuit again. The parade blockades stopped the traffic from crossing the road, but that didn't stop Speedway John.

"Hey, come back here," yelled a traffic cop.

The other vehicles behind followed him, and two motorcycle cops took off with flashing lights and sirens. The last two vehicles were pulled over, but one car remained on their tail—the black Trans Am.

"Persistent jerk," snapped John under his breath. "We have one car left, and I'm all out of options." The babies in the backseat weren't any help to his nerves when they began to awaken again and cry. Mona tried to amuse them with funny faces, but they weren't in the mood to laugh; they were hungry.

"Did we bring anything to eat?"

"No, nobody thought of food," answered Willie.

"We didn't have time either," answered John.

"Oh, that's great."

"Well, look around, Mom. Aunt Mildred always keeps snacks in the car for the boys."

"Willie, look in the glove compartment."

"Bingo," announced Willie as he opened the glove compartment and pulled out a box of animal-shaped cookies.

"Great! Quick, Willie, pass them back here."

Willie tossed the box of cookies back to Mona. She pulled out four cookies, one for each little hand, and distributed them hurriedly. Everyone was pleased with the successful cookie test because both babies stopped bawling and began gnawing ravenously. Mona shared the remainder of the cookies with the ten-year-old girl and hoped the babies would be satisfied for a while.

"Well, that's the last of the cookies, fellows. These children are starving. We're going to have to feed them someway."

John began feeling in his pockets as he remembered the food he concealed in his pockets at the Hodges's home. "Mom, take these," he announced with some relief, "maybe this will help." John handed his mother a half-eaten banana, half a bag of chips, and a partially eaten sub sandwich.

Mona glanced at the portions of food that John handed her and commented, "Thanks, John, but we're still going to need more."

"Sorry, Mom, the food helped me think so we could get away."

John made a right turn onto an intersection that fed into the main highway. Up ahead read a sign Sigsbee Stadium. "Hey, does this jingle mean anything? Listen!" John said as he began to sing, "Buy me some hot dogs and french fries, I don't care if I ever…"

Uncle Willie picked up the jingle and started singing along with John.

"Look, fellows, this is serious. We need food."

"Mom, don't you get it?"

"Get what?"

"The stadium has food."

"Oh, well, great! Let's play ball."

John looked behind him. The Trans Am was still in ardent pursuit about three car lengths behind, so he dodged in front of two big trucks that were side by side, made a sharp right turn off of the freeway, and then made another sharp turn going westward onto a side street. Instantly, John stopped the car, turned off the lights, and waited until the Trans Am passed by them. After the tailing marauder was out of sight, he turned around and drove back onto the service road. In doing so, John changed courses to an Eastward direction and zoomed off en route to the football stadium. He made his way to the stadium parking lot and parked, then everyone swiftly moved out of the car. John picked up his brother, Joey, who happened to still be asleep and walked inside. Willie took one of the babies and the little girl's hand, and Mona took the other baby.

"Mom, do you have any money?" John asked digging into his pants pockets for change.

"I guess we weren't thinking about money. Let me see," she said searching her purse for loose change. "I've got two dollars."

"Willie, how much do you have?" John asked.

Willie reached into his pockets and found fifty cents in one and a dollar in the other. "I've got a dollar and fifty cents."

"That's all? I thought mailmen carried a lot of change."

"Well, John, how much do you have?"

"I've got $7.55."

"The only reason you have more money than we do is because you got paid for a paper route you didn't do."

"Would you two pay attention to what's going on here."

"Okay, altogether we have $10.55 to spend," John announced.

"That's not a lot, considering where we are at. We'll have to make it stretch," Willie examined.

"Wait, what about tickets?" queried Mona.

"Oh, yeah, I forgot. That's not even nearly enough," announced John.

"Well, I believe that problem is solved," replied Willie. "Look, there's no one at the ticket counter. We can nonchalantly walk in, and no one will even notice."

"But that's like stealing or cheating, Willie. I can't be a part of that," Mona honestly spoke.

"Mona, you are saving the lives of all these children not to mention your own child. You could say it is for a very good cause. I guess like a donation."

"Yeah, it is for a good cause. Okay, let's go."

"Okay, GTC!" agreed John.

"GT—what?" Mona asked.

Willie and John both in unison replied, "Good 'til canceled," and laughed.

Mona wasn't sure she quite understood, but she smiled and swiftly followed behind them.

They walked inside unnoticed and ordered food for the girl and the babies, including Joey who was trying to wake up. Then they found some empty seats on the bleachers and enjoyed the last segment of the game. Even the babies enjoyed watching. They clapped their tiny food-filled hands and shouted baby gibberish along with John and Uncle Willie who were yelling at the game.

"John," Joey looked up at his elder brother.

"Hey, little brother, did you finally decide to wake up?"

"Yeah, that stuff they gave me made me a little dizzy. John, I don't want to go back there again."

"Don't worry, Joey, we won't let them or anyone else grab you ever again," John seriously spoke with assurance and a few misty-eyed tears began to form in his baby blue eyes. Joey hugged his brother. Trying to change the sadness, John reminded Joey how to defend himself. "But just remember all the kung fu playing around we've done with Uncle Willie in Mama's living room. Remember all those games we played with jump kicks and maneuvers to distract the enemy. Consider them as actual training, and apply them with real life situations, and the next time someone approaches you, be prepared to kick the snot out of 'em with all your might."

"I will, John, I will," he said with a smile and hugged his big brother again. They both smiled at each other, and John ruffled Joey's hair like their dad always did when he had a heart-to-heart talk with one of them.

Mona joined in the fun and began shouting and yelling at the game. Willie jabbed John's side moderately with his elbow and yelled in a loud yet whispering attempt in his ear, "Look at your mother. She's watching the game."

John smiled and said, "And enjoying it too." When he turned around to watch the game though, he noticed on the other side of the stadium there were two conspicuously familiar-looking characters searching the stands.

"Willie, without turning your head, shift your eyesight to the right of the field. It's them, Willie, but they haven't spotted us yet."

"Let's get out of here before they do."

"I'm right behind you."

"Mom, come on, we're going."

"Wait, it's not over yet!"

"Mom, look down below to your far right," John swayed.

"Oh, my gosh, move, move!" Mona said as she quickly grabbed the food, the baby, and briskly pushed her way off the bleachers.

"Mom," John called, "don't draw attention to us. Just walk like you're not in a hurry but walk in a hurry."

"Right."

The two men spotted them right away, and one pointed over in Mona's direction.

"There they are. Let's go!" boasted one of the men.

"Okay, now you can run," exclaimed John rushing his mother.

Mona, Willie, and John managed to escape through the exit door and quickly squeeze everyone back inside Mildred's old mustang. The babies were still happily chewing on their french fries, while the oldest child was intrigued with all the excitement.

Just as John started the engine, a loud roar came from inside. The home team won, and the crowd was in a rage to get to their vehicles first. The men that were following them slowed down and became separated within the massive crowd. By the time they forced their way out and found their cars, John was already in a line waiting to be flagged onto the main intersection.

"If we keep going like this, they'll never catch up with us." John imagined.

"Oh, no, look! One man stayed behind," Uncle Willie excitedly yelped.

John turned around in time to see the tailing vehicle driving on the right shoulder of the road a few cars back. John couldn't speed up; there were cars in front and in back of him. As he suddenly remembered passing a sign a few feet back that read "Interstate Highway 35 N," he edged his way into the far right lane and waited until he was a few feet past the exit. Slyly, hoping he wasn't seen, John then turned onto the grass and drove back to the interstate feeder road, then turned onto the Interstate 35 N highway. He drove two blocks and exited onto a two-lane road, turned down several roads, and exited onto a few highways. John turned down so many roads and highways, he eventually lost his direction.

"Fie! I believe we're lost," he said in disgust.

Uncle Willie looked around in all directions to observe the unwanted vehicle. "It doesn't matter where we are as long as we are alone."

"Don't worry." Mona tried to ease his mind. "We'll find out where we are, if you'll turn into that gas station over there."

John stopped at the gas station and went inside to seek directions. Returning with a wide smile on his face, he announced, "You're not going to believe where we are now."

"Probably the next county," answered Willie.

"Nope."

"Where are we, John?" Mona asked.

"Do you remember that little road that everybody gets lost on when they try to find our house?"

"Beaver Street?" asked Mona.

"That's the one. We're on Beaver Street. Can you believe it?"

"We can't be," Mona surprisingly questioned.

"We are."

"Are you sure it's the same Beaver Street?"

"Yes, Mom, I looked it up on the map."

"Great! Let's go home," Willie expressed happily clapping his hands, and the babies began mimicking his folly.

So John drove down Beaver Street toward home while the others relaxed and enjoyed the trip home to safety. The babies were still famished, but the french fries coated their stomachs for a little while until they drifted off to sleep. Mona hoped they would be satisfied and stay asleep until they made it back home.

From time to time, each adult would turn around and stare out the back window, hoping for the best but with fear or dread of the sight of a black Trans Am once again trailing behind.

Joey looked up at his mother and smiled sweetly. "This is a nice day," he said, shaking his little head up and down in a positive direction. Everyone laughed, and Mona hugged her son with glee.

"No, baby, this is a great day 'cause we have you back."

CHAPTER 8

HOME—A SAFE HAVEN

John felt safe when he reached sight of his home. He pulled into the driveway and opened the garage door with the remote Mildred had stowed away in the glove compartment. Slowly, he guided the car inside the garage with ease and pushed the button on the remote again to close the door behind them. The electronic sound of the closing metal doors made him feel safe even though he knew it was a misconception. John sat still thanking God for the safety of his family and especially his younger brother. He felt a sadness knowing it had to go this far to make him appreciate his brother more. John assured himself never again would he encourage anyone to run away.

While John was in deep thought, the other two adults scuffled around trying to snatch items and grab babies in an attempt to rush to the door first. Mona was the first one to enter through the kitchen door. She placed the baby down on the floor and gave him a chew toy to play with while she investigated the living room.

John, still in a solemn state of mind, sat motionless. His younger brother, Joey, reached over and pushed his shoulder. "Hey, let's go inside. I'm still hungry."

Laughing, he stated, "How can you still be hungry? You ate most of the junk food."

"There were only a few fwies left, John."

John laughed harder and replied, "Okay, let's go." Then John escorted the little girl and his brother inside the house through the kitchen entrance. As soon as the three reached the door, they could hear their mother yelling.

Loud panicked screams cried out from Mona's larynx, "John, Willie, hurry!" Because of the sudden sound of alarm that screeched from Mona's voice box, John and Willie panicked and, even though it was such a short distance, ran in the living room so fast they were practically almost out of breath. To their surprise upon arrival, the living room was in shambles. The couch cushions had been thrown into the floor in separate sectors of the room, the loveseat was toppled over on its backside, and the bookshelf was missing a handful of books that happened to be resting on the floor way across on the other side of the room. Other items were in disarray as well.

"What happened in here?" asked Willie worriedly as he picked up a downward lampstand.

Mona's emotions began to crumble as she cried out, "Willie, they got here before we did and took Josh instead." She cried with loud moans, "No! No!"

"Come on, Mona. How could they get here so fast? How could they put the pieces together that fast? Hold that thought! Mona, think about it. Even a genius detective with Internet access would take at least two to three days to know who we are and where we live. This is not their mess. Someone else did this." Willie explained the scene dramatically trying to relieve Mona's mind but was beginning to doubt himself.

"Then who, Willie, who?"

"I don't know, Mona," he answered a little disturbed. "But if they took Josh, they took Mama too, unless…"

"Unless what? You mean killed her, don't you?" Mona hysterically cried.

"No, uh, I…I don't know."

"John, come with me. Let's look upstairs," Willie commanded.

"Mona, pull yourself together and look around downstairs for clues, a note, or…" he paused, "something. Mona, okay?" he yelled from the top of the stairwell.

"Okay," Mona sobbed. "I'm fine. I'm probably just overreacting."

"Probably?" Willie scoffed questioningly as he left the upstairs hallway.

Looking around, Mona tried to explain the messy room. She thought aloud to herself, "You know, they could have had a pillow fight. Yeah, right. Who am I kidding? I can just see my mother playing pillow fight with Josh. Maybe they're upstairs."

"Willie," Mona yelled up the empty staircase, "did you find anything?"

"No, Mona, not yet. Keep searching for clues!"

"What clues?" Mona asked herself and continued looking around the muddled room. Then Mona began thinking unconventional thoughts. "Oh, Lord, I can't bare anymore! Please let my mother and son be alive." Mona squatted down on the floor in front of the bay windows, bundled her knees up against her chin, and wrapped her arms around her folded legs, then began to make short sobbing sounds as she thought about her missing family members. Tears began to flow freely now. She couldn't hold them back any longer.

Mona's little son, Joey, watched from a distance and calmly walked over, placed his small palm on her back, and gave his discontented mother some assurance as he boldly spoke wisdom to her heart, "Mama, we'a get Josh back. I pwayed fo God to bwing him home safye. I'm back now. He'a come back too," he calmly spoke and shaped a large smile for his mother to see.

Mona looked up at her compassionate little son who didn't consider his own problems but was only thinking of her and his brother Josh. Trying to see through the hurdles of tears in her eyes, she smiled warmly back at him and then threw her arms around his little body. "I love you so much. You always know what to say to me."

"Mama, I missed you a yot."

"I missed you too, honey, and I'm not going to let anyone take you away from me again. I promise," Mona said looking straight into her younger son's eyes, with tears gushing down her cheeks. Joey smiled again and squeezed his mother with a tight bear hug.

"I knew you'd come fo me, Mama. That's why I didn't worwe. You shouldn't worry now 'cause you'a get Josh back. Trust God, Mama, he'll get him back for us."

Mona looked at her son with amazement and gave him a big squeeze. She knew he was right, so she tried to settle her nerves and not panic. Instead, she decided to do something constructive, so she turned off the salty waterfall streaming down her face and changed back into Mad Mama.

Looking down at her son, Joey, she asked, "Honey, are you hungry?" Joey was still smiling. He shook his head with a positive yes answer.

"Why don't you look in the refrigerator and pull out everything you can find in the way of sandwiches, and I'll be in there shortly to help you out. I have some unfinished work to do."

"Okay, Mama."

After Joey disappeared from the living room, Mona yanked up the telephone receiver and dialed 911. A 911 operator transferred her to the police department on Main Street. The person on the other end was quick and to the point.

"Hello, NYPD, Officer Sullivan speaking. How may I help you?"

"Give me Sergeant Mender now," Mona replied with a ruthless voice and direct to the point.

"Uh, yes, ma'am, one moment, please," the officer answered reluctantly and placed the call on hold.

"Lieutenant, it sounds like that crazy Melnick lady," he announced to Officer Mender.

"Okay, I'll take it in my office, bud. Thanks."

Mona waited on hold and listened to WZZY radio station's disc jockey, Johnny Diaz. "Hello out there all you crazy mamas. This next song is dedicated to you," he announced. "You are woman, yeah!" Mona listened to the song for a few minutes, and then it was interrupted shortly after with a familiar voice.

"Hello, Lieutenant Mender speaking. How may I help you?"

"Well, you can start by doing your job, Mender. I'm tired of doing it for you."

"I beg your pardon, ma'am, what…"

Mona cut him off short. She wasn't amused at his polite approach and didn't have time for sarcasm either. "I have my son, Mender, you know the one that was kidnapped."

"But how did you…"

"I went over to Ed Hodges's home and took him back, plus three other children they had dosed up with sleeping pills," Mona crassly darted.

"You did what?" Lieutenant Mender replied with questionable doubt.

"If you don't believe me, get your lazy butt over here and see for yourself."

"I'll be right over, Ms. Melnick."

"Oh, and another thing. The reason I called is because my house has been ransacked, and my other son is missing now. Do you think your people can do something about that, or do I have to go back over to the Hodges's home and get my other son back as well?"

"Ms. Melnick, don't do anything drastic. Wait until I get there and check out the evidence at hand."

"You better hurry, Mender. I'm getting impatient, and I do not intend to wait as long as I did before. This time, I'll use a real grenade. They won't mess with any of my babies anymore. I guarantee you that."

"A real grenade?" asked the lieutenant. "Uh, Ms. Melnick, I don't…uh, think, uh…a grenade? Mr. Hodges is a dangerous man, ma'am. You could get hurt if you mess with him. Please just wait for me, okay?"

"*Get hurt?*" Mona raised her voice. "I already looked death in the face! We were chased, shot at, and almost forced off the road," Mona continued raising her voice. "All I can say, Mender, is you better get over here quick 'cause I'm getting my other son back with or without your help again." Mona completed all she wanted to say and slammed the receiver down on its base.

Lieutenant Mender was baffled. "Ma'am, Mrs. Melnick, hello." He forced the receiver on the base and rushed out of his office.

Willie and John were downstairs watching Mona's performance the whole time. John looked at Willie and commented, "I'm glad she's on our side."

"GTC on that." Willie raised his eyebrows and bobbed his head in agreement.

A rattling sound was heard coming from the storm door in the living room like it was being forced open. Mona ran to the front door and bolted it quickly. Then the doorbell rang, and Mona slowly reached to turn the lock.

"Wait, Mona, wait," Willie yelled softly, "look to see who it is first."

She peered through the peek hole and turned around with an astounding discovery. "Willie, no one's out there," she whispered with fear in her voice. "Maybe it's them. Could they have followed us here?"

"No way, Mom. They couldn't have. We didn't even know where we were," disagreed John.

"Mona, keep calm," demanded Willie. "Okay, open the lock slowly."

Mona gradually attempted to unlock the chain, but before she could do so, Willie grabbed her arm to stop her.

"No! Wait!" Willie excitedly but softly exclaimed so no one on the outside could hear.

"What, Willie?" she whispered.

"We need weapons," he whispered.

"Willie, there are no weapons in this house."

"Wait, let me think," he said as he looked around the room. "Here, use this," Willie said as he vigorously yanked the cord from the wall outlet and passed a pink shaded lamp over to Mona.

"Willie, a *lamp*? You're enjoying this way too much." Mona took the awkward weapon in her right hand, released the chain, and began twisting the doorknob.

"Mona, wait!" Willie yelled softly again.

"Now what?"

"We're not ready yet. We need weapons too."

"Okay, but hurry up."

John and Willie quickly searched the living room until they found two usable attack weapons. The doorbell rang again, so Mona cautiously pulled the door ajar about an inch. This time, she was better prepared to meet the enemy. With her hand clutched tightly around the neck of the pink shaded lamp with its bottom end up and her heart pounding faster and faster by the seconds, Mona opened the door a little wider. But before she could open the door any further, a slender hand reached inside, gave a hard push, and knocked Mona directly onto the carpeted floor. Mona jumped to her knees as she tightly clutched the lamp with its bottom end still held up high in the air and slammed the door shut pushing the intruder back outside. Willie and John stood directly behind her with their arms stretched high above their heads and their hands clutched firmly to a deadly household weapon. John tightly gripped a bar stool with both hands, and Willie rigidly clustered his hands on a six-foot hat stand. Another push from the other side gave way to the door again, and a slender figure ran inside before Mona could shove it back. The slender figure turned toward the "cave man" style defenders, amazed and confused at first, then roared out loud with laughter. Willie, annoyed by the laughter, sharply looked over at Mona and headed toward Mildred, who remained dressed in her clown costume. He did a crane lift up and down motion in an attempt to teasingly pulverize the sister enemy with his deadly weapon.

Mildred laughed a scream, "Aah! I'm sorry, but you three look so hilarious in defense position with bulging toad-eyed expressions and armed with those crazy weapons. Who were you going to kill anyway, your home decorator? Wait, let me get her on the phone." Mildred laughed so hard, she fell to the floor on her knees. The flowers on her hat bobbed back and forth. Willie looked around at Mona and John, and they became hysterical too. Soon everyone was laughing, even little Joey who wandered in investigating all the loud noise.

The lighter moment of the day was soon ended when the doorbell rang the second time. Mona, John, and Willie lifted their weapons again. Mildred was amused. "What are you doing? Have you three gone berserk?"

"It could be them this time, Mildred," Mona explained.

"Them who, Mona?"

"The kidnapers. This time they took Joshua."

"What? No, they did not."

Mona turned toward Mildred. "How do you know?"

"Because Joshua has been with me for the last two hours."

"Then how did the house develop into such a chaotic mess?"

"Oh, sorry," Mildred shrieked. "I guess I panicked a little."

"A little? Try more like a lot. Wait a minute, if you have Joshua, where is he?"

"He's probably outside the door right now wondering why you shut it in his face. Open it and find out, but put down that crazy weapon. You'll scare the poor thing."

Mona opened the door and Joshua came rushing inside. "What took you so long? It's cold out there."

"I'm sorry, baby," Mona said as she smiled and hugged her youngest son. Joshua spied his missing brother during the embrace when he looked around his mother's shoulder.

"Joey!" he said surprised and ran to him. When he reached his brother, they hugged each other tightly. "I missed you so much."

"I missed you too. Come on in the kitchen and meet the kids," Joey said, and they walked off into the kitchen with their arms around each other's shoulder.

"Okay, sis, you have some explaining to do," Willie announced to Mildred.

"Yeah, Mildred," Mona agreed. "Tell me again why my house is turned upside down."

"Well, you see, after I allured the kidnapers away, they followed me to the police station. Then you guys showed up, and they went in your direction. I drove to your house to check on Mama. She was tired and wanted to go home, so I helped her gather up all her stuff. Then in the process of helping Mama out, I misplaced the keys. I looked everywhere I could think to look—in the couch, behind the couch, under the couch, and other places I thought they might have fallen."

"Go on," Mona said.

"Well, since I couldn't find the keys to the mail truck, I decided to take your car. I couldn't find your keys either, so I panicked."

"Sounds like you two have something in common," Willie scoffed.

"Go on, don't listen to him," Mona commented.

"I turned the loveseat upside down hoping I kicked the keys underneath, but they weren't there."

"Well, that explains the upside down sofa," Willie commented.

"Anyway, after all the shuffling and tossing, I finally found the truck keys."

"Where?"

"Where did I find the keys?"

"Yes." Mona shook her head up and down.

"If I tell you, promise you won't yell at me?"

"You found them in your purse, didn't you?"

"Yeah, how'd you know?"

"A hunch I guess 'cause I would've said the same thing."

"Ha, two peas in a pod," scoffed Willie again.

"You be quiet, or you'll have the peas for breakfast," retorted Mona.

"Oh, I'm scared. I'm ready, girls, come on with it. I've been through the Mad Mama test. I can do anything now."

Mona was ready to pounce on Willie, but Mildred interrupted quickly by raising her voice, "I was going to clean up when I got back, but you two beat me here."

Mona looked back at Mildred, crouched over, and bellowed out with laughter like an Australian kookaburra.

"What?" asked Willie.

"I can just see Mildred looking for the keys in that outfit?" Mona gathered more laughter in the room as each person figuratively imagined Mildred searching for the keys in her clown costume.

"Yeah, it was hard. Every time these stupid flowers got in my way, I got angrier and threw pillows across the room."

"That explains the mystery of the scattered pillows," cried Willie.

"Well, at least you got Mama home safely," Mona commented.

"Safely? Sure, that is, if you don't count the tire that exploded, spinning around on the road, and Mama freaking out! She'll never ride in that little truck again. All I could see in the rearview mirror was Mama's gray hair flying in the air and snack cakes passing each other back and forth. She told me she'd never ride with me again. I tried to tell her it wasn't my fault, but you know Mama."

"Yeah, we know Mama," agreed Willie and Mona.

"You should have seen her face, when we finally stopped skidding. She was covered from head to toe in little snack cakes and bread slices landed on top of her head and into her lap. She was beginning to look like a human sandwich. She looked so funny; her face was glued in one position with bulging eyeballs. When I pulled in front of her house, she actually kissed the ground and waved her last good-bye to me, my driving, and that little mail truck."

Mildred's story was so immensely humorous that everyone fell to the floor with contagious laughter. "Oh, I'm laughing so hard I hurt." John moaned.

The door was still partially open, and their sounds were immeasurably loud. The laughing and moaning drifted out the front door and danced all the way down the sidewalk. A police officer approached the steps slowly as he listened questionably. He wasn't sure what he was hearing. "Are they calling out in pain," he asked himself, "or are they laughing in anger?" He wasn't sure what to make of it, so he pulled out his gun and cautiously sneaked up to the door. "Are they injured? Are they being tortured?" he asked himself again. As he approached the door stoop, he stopped first and listened again. He called out, "Ms. Melnick, is everyone all right in there?"

Mona moaned and laughed harder when she saw the police officer at the door. He thrust his foot into the front door and forced it open, then pointed his weapon toward the family and asked, "Is everyone all right?"

They laughed even harder but managed to speak to the officer. "Yes, we're all fine. Come in." She laughed with a moan.

"Are you in pain?"

"No, I'm just hurting because we've laughed so hard. You wouldn't believe the enlightening experience we've just had today. Come on in and put your gun away."

"I'm here to check out that story about your other missing boy?"

"Oh, I'm sorry, we found him. With all the commotion, I forgot to call you back."

"You went back to the Hodges's house and got your other son back already?"

Everyone laughed again, and the lieutenant looked intently with unanswered questions on his perplexed face.

"Oh, no," she snickered. "It was a mistake. He was with Mildred the whole time."

The police officer looked at Mildred with a puzzling response. "Then do you still have other children here or was that a mistake as well?"

"Oh, yes, I do. I almost forgot about them," she said, turned around, and yelled, "Oh, know!" Both babies were covered from head to toe with chocolate milkshakes, chocolate cookies, golden yellow mustard, and catsup. There were opened catsup and mustard packages scattered around on the cream-colored terrazzo floor, where the babies had squeezed each package with their hands and tried to suck out its contents. This time, even officer Mender got a good hearty laugh along with everyone else in the room.

"I'll get one of our officers to come over and take the children to the station. Meanwhile, I'll need some information from the four of you."

"You're going to take these babies to the station?"

"Yes, ma'am, that's the only place we have for them to go right now. If we don't find their parents right away, they'll be taken to a home until we do."

"Mona," Mona requested for the officer to call her by name, and the officer smiled a flirtatious smile.

"But, sergeant."

"Lieutenant."

"Lieutenant? Congratulations," she said with a modest smile and blushed. "Last time we talked, you were a sergeant. That wasn't very long ago."

"No, ma'am, uh, Mona, I took the test that next day and passed it the first time."

"That's commendable."

"Thank you."

"Lieutenant, these children have been through enough frustration today. They don't need to be treated like another number or a stack of papers on someone's desk."

"I understand your sympathy, Mona, but that's all we can do for them at this time. I don't have any other options."

"Well, I do. Let them stay here until you place them back with their parents."

In the background, Uncle Willie commented, "Oh, here we go again."

"That's a nice thing for you to do for these children, Mona, but that's a big responsibility for you. Are you sure you want to handle this right now? I mean, all of you have been through a lot yourselves."

"I'm sure."

"Okay, I'll have to call my captain and get an approval." The lieutenant walked over to the phone, dialed a number, and was transferred to Captain Cornelius. He explained the story and walked into another room for privacy as he spoke a few minutes longer. Lieutenant Mender walked back into the room, placed the phone back on its base, and commented to Mona, "I'm waiting for him to call back with an answer."

"Okay. Well, is anyone hungry? I'm famished."

"Yeah, you know I am," answered Willie, "that food we had wasn't enough to feed even two of us."

"It was hardly enough to feed the children," Mona agreed. "I know those babies are starving. They acted like they hadn't eaten for three days."

"Kidnapers don't usually feed the children very much food because the children have a tendency to get sick," Lieutenant Mender stated.

"That's true! I overheard Mr. Hodges's secretary talking about it when I was hiding inside one of the upstairs bedrooms," Mona announced.

Lieutenant Mender looked over at her with a shocked expression upon his face. "You were inside his home?"

Mona smiled slightly and answered reluctantly, "Ye-ah."

John walked into the kitchen and opened the refrigerator. To his surprise, the shelves were bare. Then he bellowed out to his mother as he walked toward the living room, "Mom, the fridge is empty. You're gonna have to go to the store."

"Okay, then I'll make a quick dash to the corner store to pick up some cold cuts, milk, and fresh bread. Would anyone like to add anything else to the list?" No one had an additional food item to add to Mona's list, so Mona grabbed her purse and headed toward the front door, then turned around and faced Willie and John.

"Are you two able to hold down the day care until I get back?"

"Not a problem," Willie said, and John agreed.

Before Mona could open the front door, Joey ran to her side and tugged at her sleeve. "Mama," Joey asked, "can I go with you, pwease?"

Mona hesitated a moment. "Baby, maybe you better stay here. I don't want to lose you again."

"Pwease, I won't yet anyone take me this time. I promise."

She looked over at Willie, who happened to be making arguable faces, and slowly commented, "But I guess I'll have to get use to taking you with me sooner or later, huh? It might as well start now." Willie shook his head in agreement and smiled at Mona. "Okay, come on, but stay close by me and scream, kick, and even bite if someone even looks at you."

"Okay, Mama, they won't get me this time. I know how to fight back. John explained it to me."

Mona smiled at Joey, and they walked out the front door but turned around and walked back inside. "Wrong way," she said, "the van's in the garage." She and Joey marched through the kitchen and exited the garage door to get to Mona's minivan.

During their absence, Lieutenant Mender managed to gather a group of female officers to take care of the children. John was quite amiable to one young lady with red hair. He followed her to the kitchen and helped out as much as possible.

"Your family did a dangerous thing. You must be very brave or stupid," commented the red-haired police officer.

"What would you do, if your brother was kidnapped? Leave him behind?"

"Oh, no, I think what you did was great!"

"You do?"

"Oh, yeah!"

"But you just called us stupid."

"I didn't mean you are stupid, I meant…I don't know what I meant. I just know you must be very brave to do what you did," she said, kissed him quickly, and rushed out the door. John tried to follow her, but she was busy being given orders by Lieutenant Mender. She turned and smiled at John as she rushed back to the kitchen to gather up the babies for bathing.

"Here, let me help you," he said, and they both grabbed a toddler and proceeded toward one of the bedrooms.

Lieutenant Mender watched as they dove-eyed each other and shook his head. "Great," he said underneath his breath, "a day care and a dating service all in one quick phone call. What could be better than that?"

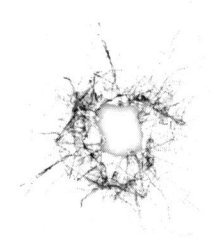

CHAPTER 9

THE STORE STALKER

Mona and Joey climbed into the minivan and headed eastward down the street toward the nearest store that was open. The twenty-four-hour Jones Market was only a few blocks down from Mona's house, so it just took five to ten minutes to drive there. Mona circled the parking lot trying to locate the nearest place to park. Being satisfied with the closest space available, she parked, and they jumped out together side by side.

Mona walked inside the store with Joey clutched close to her side. As they walked toward the refrigerated section of the store, Joey continued to cling to his mother like melted butter on toast. He was as much afraid to leave her side, as she was his. Without a moment's notice, Mona quickly opened the glass door and handed four different varieties of cold cuts over to Joey to place into the shopping basket. She stopped and looked in all directions like a secret agent and moved on down the refrigerated section of the store. As she reached inside for a gallon of milk, a body brushed against her back and darted to the next aisle. Mona stopped, turned to look around her, and then released the door handle allowing it to close shut abruptly making a loud banging noise. Joey jumped and shivered with fear. Cautiously veering down each aisle she approached, Mona reached the bread, cake, and pastry shelves.

"Joey," she whispered, "I believe someone's watching us. Stay close and hold onto my blouse."

"Mama, yet's go home. I'm not hungry anymore."

"It's all right, honey. Just stayed glued to my side."

As she turned the corner, a strange old man grabbed Joey's arm. Joey screamed and began kicking. Mona turned and, without thinking, kicked him face down to the floor dropping the gallon of milk that splattered when it hit the floor, and the white liquid ran out everywhere. The man lay lifeless on the floor. People came from every corner of the store to see what happened. A newspaper reporter, who followed her into the store, took pictures of the whole scene unnoticed by Mona. She was too frightened by the attack.

The old man reached up his left hand that was clutching a green lollipop. Out of breath, he managed to ask with puzzlement, "Is he a diabetic? Or something?"

Mona was embarrassed. She helped the elderly man to his feet and tried to explain her responsive reaction. The man assured her that he understood as he limped to the checkout stand and sat down in a chair behind the counter.

"Oh, I'm okay, lady. Ain't no woman able to kick me and keep me down," he said holding his back. "I'm Larry Jones, the manager of this store. You take whatever you need, it's on the house."

"I can't do that, Mr. Jones, especially after what I did to you."

"Aah, don't let it bother you. You did what you thought was right, Mona. If that happened to me, I'd probably be touchy too. You go finish shopping, and I'll keep an eye on this little man." Mona hesitated at first. "Go on. Don't worry. He'll be all right with me. And don't worry about the spill. I'll get Gerta May to give me a hand with it."

Feeling a little more at ease, she turned toward the cooler and grabbed another gallon of milk, four loaves of bread, and some pastries off the shelf and stuffed them in a small shopping carrier. The whole time Mona kept looking toward Joey to make sure he was still safe. While she gathered the remaining items from her shopping list, Mona watched cautiously as Joey talked to the elderly man. Joey maintained a watchful eye on his mother as well. He continued looking back in her direction to make sure she was still there.

"Awe you okay, mista?" Joey asked. "My mom kicked you pwetty hawd."

"Oh, I'm all right, son. You know your Mama must love you very much."

"She does. She got me back from those bad people. They made me sweep too much."

"Sweep?"

"I can't say it very kearye. You know go to bed."

"Oh, you mean sleep."

"Right."

Mona completed all her shopping and tried to pay the grocery clerk for all her goods, but he refused to accept her money. "It's on the house," he said. "You come and shop with us all you want and bring that little man with you. He'll always be safe in this store. I'll see to that," he said as he grabbed a gun from a secret shelf.

"Wow! Thank you, Mr. Jones," she said. "Mr. Jones, earlier you commented all that I've been through. How do you know what I've been through? And how do you know my name?"

"Oh, honey, you're all over the news. Everyone knows your story. Mona Melnick, you're a hero."

"A hero? Oh, no, that means the kidnappers know now. I've got to get home quick. Thanks again, Mr. Jones," Mona said as she and Joey dashed out the door.

"Just call me Larry."

"Okay, Larry, have a great day and thanks again for everything."

One step out the door and lights and cameras were flashing from every direction in front of them. Reporters were clicking their cameras, trying to get cheap shots of Mona and her son as they exited the store. Police officers with flashing lights were stationed outside the store waiting for Mona to make her purchases. They escorted her and Joey to the minivan and followed them back to her home. When Mona returned to the house, there were TV news reporters and cameramen on her front lawn. People from the neighborhood were out on the streets trying to find the scoop on Mona's popularity. She was totally amazed, but feared the life of her family now that their home address was exposed all over the television and the newspapers. Mona pushed her garage door genie and drove into the garage, quickly releasing the door after she entered. She and Joey jumped out with the groceries and headed for the kitchen entrance. A news reporter that snuck in unnoticed advanced her as she approached the kitchen door. "Aah!" Mona yelled with surprise. "Get him out of here."

Police officer Renardo Bengeti pulled out his gun and pointed it at the man. "Okay, mister, take your camera and go quickly, or I'll have to shoot you."

Willie grabbed the man's arm and led him to the front door. "They're serious about this, man. You better get out of here. You'll get a statement when everyone else gets one," he said as he abruptly pushed the man out the front door and rapidly slammed it shut.

"What's going on?" Mona asked inquisitively.

"You don't know?"

"Why, am I supposed to? Am I missing something?"

"Mona, everyone knows about the scene at the grocery store," Willie announced.

"What? How? It just happened."

"News travels fast around this neighborhood, Mad Mama," Lieutenant Mender commented. "You're quite a celebrity. When Hodges was arrested for kidnapping, your name came up. It's all over the news. Newspaper reporters took off on the story. Not only did you retrieve your kidnapped son but also three other missing children as well. The people are calling you a hero."

"Yeah, Mom, they filmed your kick live on national television."

"What? How do you know that?"

"We just watched it."

"What? You saw me on television."

John snidely laughed. "Yeah, it was great."

"Great? That's just great," Mona commented disgustingly and walked into the kitchen to make sandwiches.

"Lieutenant," she yelled, "did you have any luck finding the parents?"

"Mona, just call me Bob," he said and followed her into the kitchen.

"Okay, Bob." She smiled.

"In answer to your question, we've located two sets of parents, but the last one is a puzzler. She's not even listed on the missing children's report."

"Surely, by now she would be missed," Mona spoke with concern as she handed the lieutenant a sandwich.

"That's what we thought, but apparently, no one knows she's missing, and we don't have any clues where to complete our search."

"Did you try other states?" Mona asked.

Lieutenant Mender nodded yes as he was munching on a sandwich and after swallowing said, "Mona, we've tried every angle possible, but no leads."

Mona became emotional while she continued spreading mayonnaise on each piece of bread she had piled up to create sandwiches for the hungry group. "Lieutenant, Bob, what have I done? My family's lives are in danger now because of me? What am I going to do?" Mona sobbed, trying to hold back the tears, but they began gushing forth.

"Mona," the lieutenant spoke softly as he tenderly touched her left shoulder, "you don't have anything to worry about. Your family will be safe. I'll see to it myself."

"You promise?" she asked being reassured by his touch.

The lieutenant reached over and turned Mona's body around toward him; this time, he grabbed both shoulders. "Yes, I promise. I'm not going to let anything happen to you or any member of your family." Mona laid her head on Bob's shoulder, and he embraced her tightly with his comforting arms.

The phone interrupted their conversation with a loud, bursting tone. Mona lifted her head, and Lieutenant Mender picked up the receiver that was housed in the pocket of his right belt clip, then with a quick hello listened a few minutes before answering again.

"Hold on a minute, Lou, okay."

Lieutenant Mender took a moment to speak to Mona, before completing his phone call, "Are you okay?"

"I'm all right. Thanks for listening."

"I'm here any time," he said tenderly concerned with a smile, "but I've got to take this call. Hang on, okay?"

Mona tried to smile back, grabbed the plate of sandwiches she had finished compiling, and walked out of the kitchen to distribute the munchies to all the hungry people in the room. Lieutenant Mender continued with his phone conversation and followed behind her. Of course, the plate Mona was holding almost became empty in seconds as every person grabbed a sandwich like wolves devouring their meal. Mona took the sandwiches that she cut into small squares for the little ones and placed one in each hand. Lieutenant Mender watched Mona as she played with the children.

"You're not gonna believe this, Lieutenant," said the voice on the other end waiting for a response.

"Try me. I'll believe anything today."

"We got a disturbance call from a tenant in an apartment complex out on the south side of the mall. It seems her neighbor was beating on her living room wall."

"Yeah, so?"

"Well, when we checked it out, the neighbor was tied to a kitchen chair and locked inside his closet. He began beating the wall to get the neighbor's attention."

"I still don't see the connection."

"Well, we found a military ball cap in this man's closet with the name Joey marked on the underside part of the bill."

"Yeah, and?"

"The ball cap turns out to be the missing child's cap."

"Really."

"That's not all. Get this. He kept saying Mad Mama and her gang did this to him. He described them fully. The Mama was wearing a green military outfit heavily armed with artillery, one member of the gang was wearing a postman's uniform, another was wearing a leather jacket, and the other one was wearing a clown suit with three flowers growing out of the hat."

"A clown?" Lieutenant Mender excitedly raised his voice. Then he turned and looked in the direction of four would-be desperadoes—Mona in her green military camouflage attire, John in his leather pants including leather jacket, Willie with his postman's uniform, and Mildred dressed as a clown wearing a hat with three bobbing flowers. Their apparel was the same dress as the officer described on the phone.

"Anyway," the officer continued, "we got him for kidnapping. He confessed to everything. Lieutenant, he kept saying, 'Don't let Mad Mama get me.'"

"Mad Mama, huh? Okay, thanks, Lou. You guys did a great job."

Everyone in the room was listening to the conversation. "What did he say, Lieutenant?" Mona queried with innocence.

"Enough," the lieutenant replied. "I don't know what you four did in the last forty-eight hours, and I don't want to know, but you must have really been one desperate bunch to pull off such an escapade. I'm surprised you're still alive."

"Whatever do you mean?" Mona questioned innocently again.

"Oh, I think you know what I mean, Mad Mama," the lieutenant toyed with Mona's thoughts.

Mona smiled, shrugged her shoulders, and changed the subject. "Anybody for seconds? I'm still hungry," she said and walked back to the kitchen to make more sandwiches.

"Yeah, I'm famished," answered Willie. The rest of the desperado bunch followed behind and laughed in a huddle as they reached the kitchen. Lieutenant Mender turned his head and smiled, shaking his head in disbelief.

The desperadoes hung up their costumes for the day and entertained the children while waiting for the parents to arrive and collect them. The day grew old, and night began to darken the sky. The wait seemed long and tiring, but the families finally came and left. Each offered Mona a reward, but she refused to take their money. She only replied, "I have my reward," as she reached over to her middle son, Joey, and held him in her arms tenderly. Even so, the families offered her anything she wanted or needed at any time.

"Well, one more left," commented the lieutenant. "Will it be all right with you, Mona, if she stays for the night?"

"Sure. Did they find her parents?"

"You'll find out first thing in the morning. I'll have an officer bring you the newspaper."

"You're going to have an officer drive all the way over here in the morning just to bring me a newspaper?"

"No. There will be officers stationed outside your front door, your side door, and your back door all night long."

"That many?"

"Mona, you're in a dangerous situation right now."

"Did they catch any of the criminals that took Joey?"

"We have Mr. Hodges and some of his men, but there are others out there that would like to see you and your gang disappear. You're not safe. You know you'll have to be placed in a secure area until all this blows over."

"You mean the Witness Protection Program, don't you?"

"Yeah. Ben Hodges will try every way possible to kill you and your family so you can't testify. He has many friends, if you call them friends, outside the prison system."

"Okay, I guess we don't have a choice."

"Not if you want to live."

"But where will we go?"

"I'm not sure what they have decided, but I'll let you know as soon as I know."

Mona half-smiled and announced, "Well, I guess I better put the kids to bed."

Mona walked over to the little girl. "Come on, sweetie," she said as she reached her arm around the little girl's back.

"Oh, that's all right, Ms. Melnick, I'll tuck her in. That's my job for tonight," explained Cindy, the young redheaded nurse, who was sent over to help with the children.

"Wait, I'll help you," eagerly announced John.

Mona watched as John rushed to lead the way. "He's never been that eager to help out before," she reflected.

Willie and Mildred offered to put Mona's other two children down for the night, leaving Lieutenant Mender and Mona alone in the room. "That was easy enough," she commented.

"It's nice to have help sometimes, isn't it?"

"Yeah, very nice. I'm so use to doing everything myself."

"I can tell."

"Bob, will you be here tonight? For some reason, I feel safer when you're around."

"I'll be here for a little while, but I have to get back to the station to fill out paperwork. Don't worry, I'll be checking in on you," he said as he thought a moment. "Mona, those officers outside are well-trained to do their job. You don't have anything to worry about."

"I know."

"Why don't you get some rest? I'll lock up for you."

"Okay, thanks."

"Mona?" he said tenderly.

"Yeah."

"Oh, nothing," he said afraid to ask the question.

"What, Bob? You can ask me anything."

"Oh, well, I was just wondering if you'd have lunch with me after this is all over?"

"Yes, I would like that very much, but are you sure you can handle having lunch with a notorious desperado?"

He smiled and added, "I think I can handle a beautiful woman like you."

Mona blushed and smiled back. Lieutenant Mender looked into Mona's eyes and softly stroked her face with his hand. "You're an amazing woman," he said. "I know it took a lot of love and courage to do what you and your family did, and to bring back those other children is very commendable. You could have easily left them behind," he said as he reached down and kissed her forehead. Then he kissed her softly on the lips, and the taste of Mona's lips was so addictive that he had to embrace her lips again. The compassionate kiss lasted longer than he expected. "I'm sorry, I guess I shouldn't have done that. I am on duty."

"I'm glad you did," Mona replied. "It's very comforting to know that our police officers know how to handle all types of situations, even sensual ones." She smiled and started to walk away, but Bob grabbed her arm, pulled her back into his arms, and kissed her again.

"Don't leave," she whispered softly.

"Don't worry, I'll be back," he said, kissed her again, and turned toward the door, holding her hand. The officer stopped, turned around, and announced, "I'll be back tomorrow. You can count on that," he said as he lifted her hand and kissed it gently.

"I am counting on that. I'll be right here eagerly waiting," she illusively commented with a sensuous smile, then turned and walked toward her bedroom for the night.

After reinforcing all the windows and doors, Lieutenant Mender returned to the station. Mona's last remark kept drifting back into his mind as he completed all the unfinished paperwork. He couldn't get her out of his mind, but the lieutenant knew this was only the beginning of paperwork to keep this family alive, so he worked late into the night to completely erase the memories of the Melnick family.

Later that night, Lieutenant Mender drove by Mona's house one last time, before he retired for the evening. He wanted to make sure mischief was not at hand and the Melnick family was safe.

CHAPTER 10

MONA'S SURRENDER TO PEACE

Mona rolled the covers back and lay down on her king-sized mattress. Thinking all was over, she assuredly thought going to sleep and resting soundly would be easy now. Instead, she rolled around all night reliving the horrifying events that actually took place only yesterday. They continued tormenting her mind all through the night nightmare after nightmare, as they had previously.

Being annoyed of the lack of sleep she acquired, Mona sprang up from her sleigh bed, threw off the downy-filled comforter, and promptly headed down the hallway toward the kitchen about twenty feet away. When she entered the kitchen, Mona promptly filled the coffee pot with water, some even measures of ground coffee, and plugged it into a nearby outlet. "I just don't understand why I'm still having nightmares. Maybe when the newspaper gets here, I can read and clear my mind." Mona tried convincing her brain so the thoughts that kept her sleep in disarray would vanish.

Mona looked at the clock. It read 5:00 a.m. "I've never been up this early," she mumbled to herself. Mona still insisted on essaying to relax and enjoy her usual morning tryst with God, so she filled a mug with steaming hot coffee, doctored it with cream and sugar, and marched confidently into the living room. Standing back inside the shadows, Mona gazed out of the bay windows, as if she were in a trance. Waiting for the sunrise to burst out its inspirational glow, she tried to focus on pleasant remembrances while pushing back the unwanted ones, but they continued to fester her mind.

"I just don't get it! Why am I still having yesterday's feedbacks? It is over, isn't it?"

As Mona continued to watch the dim silence outside, she focused her eyes on the morning paper as it was tossed into her front yard. "Finally," Mona said taking a deep breath, opened the front door, and stepped out onto the sidewalk. Firmly tightening a grip on the handle of the coffee mug she was holding, Mona sipped some of the hot brew. A mist of steam brushed against her face, and a cold chill rushed throughout Mona's entire body as she walked outside into the frosty morning to retrieve the paper in hopes of also relieving her mind.

"Morning, ma'am," greeted Officer Hunt as he reached down to retrieve the paper and handed it to Mona.

"Morning. I suppose you were given watch duty this morning," she answered and took the paper from his hand.

"Yes, ma'am, but actually I've been here most of the night," answered Hunt. "My relief will be here in about an hour."

"I bet you're tired."

"Not really. You get use to it." He stayed close by and waited for Mona to go back inside before he walked back to his squad car.

"Oh, ma'am? Lieutenant Mender said for you and your whole family to be ready to move at 0800 this morning," he said remembering.

"Move? I don't understand."

"The Witness Protection Program requires you to move, immediately."

"Oh, that quick?"

"Yes, ma'am. Just pack what you need. We'll have movers come in and pack everything else."

"Okay, thanks, Officer."

"You're welcome, ma'am. Oh, one more thing."

Mona turned around slightly. "Yes?"

"I just want you to know I think what you did for those other children was great. You could have left them behind, and they would have made millions off those children."

Mona turned completely around toward the officer and asked, "Millions? Were they famous?"

"You could say that. Both of them belonged to movie stars."

"They weren't picked up by anyone I know."

"No, they were picked up by police personnel for safety reasons."

"Oh, but they acted like they were the parents. They even offered me an award."

"Yeah, the real parents conveyed the message. That part was real, but the parents were police officers. We couldn't take any chances."

"What about the little girl?"

"Oh, you haven't heard about that one yet, have you?"

"No, why? Just open the paper, ma'am. You're gonna love this morning's edition."

"I will? Why?"

"Just read it. We're waiting for your response."

"You're waiting for my response? You guys are watching me?"

"Yes, ma'am."

"Are you the only ones left?" Mona noticed all the policemen were gone, except for a squad car parked out front.

"No, ma'am, there's one more out back and three officers posted around your house," he said as he turned and walked away.

"Officer," she yelled, "would you guys like some coffee?"

"Oh, no thank you, ma'am, we brought our own."

"Okay, I guess you came prepared." Mona waved at the other officers in the squad car, and they waved back; then, Mona returned inside the house.

"Yes, ma'am, as always."

Grabbing the morning edition of the *Sun Valley Newspaper* that she had been clutching underneath her arm, Mona opened it hoping to introduce new thoughts and read away her problems. Mona viewed the picture on the first page and secretly gasped, "Oh, my gosh!" To her amazement, there she stood, the cover story, wearing her camouflage green military attire, heavily armed from head to toe and in a high kick position. Then suddenly, like a faucet that couldn't be turned off, the unwanted flashbacks began gushing forth, surfacing so quickly they seemed to be out of control. Mona began to worry.

"Get a grip, Mona," she commanded herself as flashbacks continued to haunt and tease her, "it's over. The kids are gone, except for one, and the kidnappers are in custody. What could I be missing?"

Finally, what she had longed for just arrived. The premature morning opened the new day with a warm, glowing light that pierced its way through the bay windows of Mona's two-story home. As she stood back within the silhouettes and watched, the rays of the warm sunlight stretched forth into her home and eased her mind. Then the horizon lit up with a golden spray with pink and blue highlights that surrounded the skies.

This looks like it's going to be another wonderful day, thought Mona, and for a brief time, Mona relaxed and enjoyed the scenic view. "I don't know what I was worried about. I'm already feeling release." Then Mona began reading the story underneath her picture and gasped as she read each line. Her peaceful sunrise turned sour when once again recollections of yesterday pushed back into her thoughts.

"That was real? I actually did that…and with a grenade? Oh, my baby! Oh, please, I don't want to relive this again," she said to herself pausing in between each sentence. Yesterday's memories were too disturbing for Mona's mind to stay serene. "I must have been mad and out of my mind," she continued. "I risked the lives of my family and my children. How did it get so far out of control?" she wondered incessantly. "And why won't my mind let go of these past events? It's over, isn't it?"

With her eyes staring up into the heavens, she cried aloud, yet softly as to not awaken her family, "God, is there a reason why I'm suppose to keep remembering all this? Maybe it's not over yet. Maybe I missed something. What could it be? Tell me, please."

The officers outside the house watched intently, a couple held up binoculars, and all waited for Mona's reaction as she continued reading the morning edition of the *Sun Valley Newspaper*. Then came the expression everyone was waiting for when Mona read the title of the cover page. Her eyes bulged out like a bullfrog, and her mouth dropped open wide enough to insert a foot-long sandwich when she read the headlines—"MAD MAMA MELNICK NAPS KIDNAPPER'S KID! see page 2." Gasping for air with spilled coffee everywhere, Mona screamed so loud she woke up John and Willie.

Quickly running down the stairs, John and Willie almost tripped over each other. "What's wrong, Mona?" asked Willie.

"Mom, are you okay?"

Still confused and wildly agitated Mona looked at John with tearful eyes and then turned to her brother Willie. She cried, "That girl in there belongs to the kidnapper! We're kidnappers!"

"Mona calm down," Willie spoke trying to soothe Mona's emotional stress.

"How do you know that?" queried John.

"Look," she spoke with exasperation as she thrust the paper toward them, "it's on the front page!"

Willie and John grabbed the newspaper together and began reading the story. "I don't believe it," answered Willie.

"No wonder we couldn't find the girl's parents," announced John, "they were locked up."

"Well, that puzzle finally connected its last piece," Willie spoke.

"I wonder where she will go," John retorted.

"She probably will be given over to a close relative until her parents get out of prison," Willie commented.

"Poor child," Mona passionately commented, "none of this was her fault, and she has to be punished."

"Yeah, but there's nothing we can do about it, Mona, you know that, right?" said Willie.

"I know, Willie, I just feel sorry for her."

Mona turned and looked at Willie. "Willie, she…"

"No, Mona, I know what you're thinking. I am sure the girl has other relatives who can care for her."

"Yeah, I guess you're right."

Mona peered out the bay windows again and glanced over at the police car. "I guess they got a good laugh out of all this," she said as she noticed the officers roaring with laughter.

"You're the highlight of their evening, Mona. Not everyone gets to meet the notorious Mad Mama Melnick."

Willie and John laughed and waved at the police officers. Mona politely smiled and waved back too.

"Come on, John," commanded Willie, "help me get something to clean up this coffee that Mad Mama spilled out all over the floor. Imagine, she can escape from hoodlums, but she can't hold her coffee." They laughed and walked away, leaving Mona standing in the room still amazed.